THE KINDLY ONE

AND OTHER HORRIFIC TALES

Other titles by
Danielle Ackley-McPhail

THE ETERNAL CYCLE SERIES
Yesterday's Dreams
Tomorrow's Memories
Today's Promise

THE ETERNAL WANDERINGS SERIES
Eternal Wanderings

THE BAD-ASS FAERIE TALE SERIES
The Halfling's Court
The Redcap's Queen
The High King's Fool
(forthcoming)

Baba Ali and the Clockwork Djinn
(with Day Al-Mohamed)

The Literary Handyman
Build-A-Book Workshop
More Tips From the Handyman

The Ginger KICK! Cookbook

SHORT FICTION
A Legacy of Stars
Transcendence
Consigned to the Sea
Flash in the Can
The Fox's Fire
The Die Is Cast
(with Mike McPhail)

THE KINDLY ONE

AND OTHER HORRIFIC TALES

DANIELLE ACKLEY-MCPHAIL

Pennsville, NJ

PUBLISHED BY
Paper Phoenix Press
A division of eSpec Books
PO Box 242
Pennsville, NJ 08070
www.especbooks.com

ISBN: 978-1-949691-75-7
ISBN (ebook): 978-1-949691-74-0

Interior Design: Danielle McPhail
Cover Art: Beautiful Woman Occultist © Warm_Tail,
             www.shutterstock.com
Cover Design: Mike McPhail
Copyediting: Greg Schauer

DEDICATION

To my good friend, James Chamber.
It was only a matter of time...

CONTENTS

THE KINDLY ONE

Guilt, the venom running through humanity's veins,
The cancer eating mankind's soul.
Death, both courted and earned, well fed upon denial.

DUST ROSE IN A ROOSTER'S PLUME ON THE HORIZON LONG BEFORE there was anything to see on the road. Something big was coming in... something bigger than the usual transport bus.

Callie Dupree watched as Warden Schmidt strode across the compound with purpose, his expression twisted into twenty kinds of pissed off. Guards trailed him out the building until three times the normal detail paced the wall, clustered in the towers, and stood positioned around the compound. Each one ran hands unconsciously along the stocks of their rifles or the lengths of their nightsticks. The warden's gaze slid from the crowded Yard to his men. He tensed further when his eyes locked on the approaching dust cloud. He swore as he headed for the main gate. "A bit more ga'damn warning would have been decent."

Near-forgotten in the Yard, the inmates wandered toward the fence that ran along the dead zone between their enclosure and the road that crossed the prison perimeter. They milled in a loose throng,; their attention riveted on the goings-on. They gathered as close as they could to the barrier without touching the charged links. For once none of them paid attention to turf or boundaries. Everyone was too caught up in the tension hanging in the air thicker than the desert heat.

The warden lifted a walkie to his lips and handsets squawked all over the compound. Callie edged closer to a nearby guard, trying to hear what was going on. An acrid tang wafted from the young kid in his all-too-new uniform. His dull, dirt-brown hair hung in damp hanks over his forehead and his eyes were black and shocky. He jerked as the warden's voice came hard and flat over the handset. "Weapons at the ready, the Feds are bringin' her in."

Callie's cheek ticked. She carefully worked herself away, watching as the guard cocked his weapon, his hands trembling. She recognized the look on his face—after fifteen years on the inside she'd seen it plenty enough. This one was likely to do something stupid. She was not going to be anywhere within range when that happened. Instead, she worked her way across the yard to Joelle's side.

"Someone new is being brought in. Got half of them wired enough to piss themselves." Callie murmured, her face neutral and her eyes half closed in cultivated boredom. She pushed a length of steel-grey hair behind her ear, revealing ghostly track scars up and down her arm before tucking her thumbs into the waistband of her prison-issue jeans.

"Yeah, and the other half enough to open full bore." Joelle spit in disgust. "They couldn't do this a week from fuckin' now, could they? They're gonna be agitated for months, breathin' down our neck every damn second. I hate the bitch already."

The warning claxon sounded, cutting off further comment. The two women turned with the others; eyes trained on the approaching vehicles. The caravan consisted of a dark, official-looking sedan, followed by a semi, which was then followed by another sedan.

This was not the usual prisoner transfer. Murmurs of speculation buzzed the air like locusts. They cut off a mere moment later. The semi sped up recklessly, weaving the width of the road, the trailer swaying dangerously behind. There was a screech of metal on metal and the squeal of tires skewing sideways on the asphalt as the truck zoomed past the lead sedan, clipping it in passing. There were gasps and yells as the government car peeled off into the sagebrush, smoke pouring from the front end, airbag powder clouding the inside.

Half the guards boiled out of the gatehouses and towers like ants out of a collapsing mound. The rest maintained their posts. All of them had their weapons raised and trained on the semi barreling through the gate. Twenty feet of electrified fence wrapped around the cab, arcing and sparking like Fourth-of-July fireworks. The guards in the truck's path scrambled behind the jersey wall that ran along the asphalt parallel to the security fence. Brakes squealed until the tires smoked thick, black, acrid smoke. At the same time, the engine revved.

Callie was close enough to see the expression on the driver's face. He was paler than chalk and his eyes burned just this side of madness. For a second, she figured he was not going to halt the rig at the inner security gate either. It was almost a disappointment when the truck came to a whiplash stop a few feet before another collision. The second sedan fishtailed to a halt behind it, blocking the breached gate as well as it was able to. Feds poured out the far side and positioned themselves with guns braced on their car as they used it for cover.

The trucker forced his door open against the twisted fence tangled with the front of his truck. The frantic babble drifting out of the compartment sent shivers up Callie's spine. Beside her, Joelle went dead still.

"Damn..." Callie drew the word out long and low, her gut turning over in a hard knot. "Who do they have in the back, Satan's mother or something?"

The guy scrambled from the truck and staggered toward the group behind the barrier. Feds and guards alike barked for him to drop to the ground where he was. He acted as if he did not hear them, listening, as he was, to whatever went on in his head. A second warning rang out, also ignored.

"Oh crap!" Callie yelled. "Down!" About three quarters of the inmates listened, including Joelle. The air exploded with revolver fire and the crack of the guards' rifles. They took the driver down.

It should have ended there, one man on the ground.

There was a strangled moan to Callie's right. She looked up and all she could see was the raised rifle of the young guard she'd noticed earlier, his eyes wide and his knuckles white against the barrel and stock. Boom! Boom! *Chi-chink...* Boom! Boom! She ducked once more as bullets ricocheted off the metal trailer into the Yard. There was the thud of more bodies hitting the ground. Both men and women screamed; anger, fear, and pain rose in an unholy chorus.

"For chrissake! Hold your fire!" The warden's voice cut through the chaos. "Someone relieve that fool of his weapon!"

Callie lifted her eyes from the dirt and scanned the compound. The Feds were positioning themselves around the truck and driver. Half of the guards had their weapons trained on the semi, a handful pinned the trigger-happy guard to the ground, and the rest were split between tending the wounded and covering the inmates.

Someone whispered, "The sins of the father... madness demands madness."

Callie tried to see who, but no one was near enough that she should have been able to hear them, except for Joelle, and she had not said a word. A shiver traveled from Callie's neck to the tips of her limbs and she looked toward the circle of guards.

The truck driver lay crumpled on the concrete, his blood spreading around him like a flamenco dancer's skirts. He still babbled, though the words grew fainter. "Get outa my head... can't judge me... no... didn't do nothin'... didn't touch... didn't mean nothin'... talkin' ain't illegal... outa my head... shut up!" his dimming gaze flickered back and forth from the truck to the guards huddled around him, his expression frantic and pleading. A final whisper slipped from between his lips. "Save... me."

Across the compound, the young guard twitched where he lay, his expression in a state of constant flux, his sanity in shards. Callie suppressed a shiver and turned her eyes away. She climbed to her feet with utmost caution. Joelle scrambled up next to her. All around them, others stood in stunned silence.

One of the Feds stepped forward. "Warden Schmidt? You need to clear the area."

Behind him, the rest of the government men were securing the zone, dealing with the dead body and the crazed guard, several waited by the trailer's rear doors. The guards were already herding the inmates out of the Yard. Callie trailed back as much as she could get away with, trying to catch a glimpse of whatever monster required an entire, heavy-duty tractor trailer and several carloads of G-men to bring her in.

"Move it!" one of the guards growled. *Whack!* Callie caught a club across the shoulder. She gritted her teeth and kept silent, but Joelle was still by her side and she had the devil in her eye.

"Bet you hate turnin' that in at the end of the day," Joelle tossed back at the guard in a deceptively causal tone. Her gaze trailed down the length of him. "Must be like castration, seeing as that's more equipment than what you got dangling."

The guard got in a good backhanded slam across her kidneys with the nightstick before another guard stepped in.

"Yo, man," he murmured. "Not with the Feds here."

Callie hauled Joelle away before anyone else decided to take any kind of shot. "What do you think you're playin' at?"

Joelle's gaze was flat and cold, with something else flickering deep behind barriers nearly as good as Callie's own. Somehow Joelle managed to give off the impression of sneering without lifting her lip. She was good at that.

"Hey, he got off your case, didn't he?" She blinked and gave the barest lift of her shoulder.

Callie practically felt a tick mark go down on the negative side of her mental tally of debts owed. Every muscle tensed and she dropped her hand from Joelle's arm. With practiced ease, she invaded Joelle's personal space and captured the young woman's eye from right up close, leaving no room for misunderstanding. She let her own expression go heavy and hard. "Don't pull that kind of crap again, I take my licks. I haven't fought my way through fifteen years of permanent residence for some young punk like you to make me out as weak in front of *anyone.* I'm already in for life; you do one more thing that threatens to cut my sentence short and I'll take you out myself."

Joelle went very still. Her jaw twitched and her expression went blank, but her eyes burned. They had a bit of a stare-down that Callie had no trouble holding until Joelle's gaze flickered away. As far as she was concerned, the debt of moments ago had been discharged when Callie gave the girl fair warning.

"Yeah, whatever," Joelle blew her off. "They're heading us to the Mess, *Mama.* Guess they're dishin' lunch early."

Mama. Callie suppressed a shudder. She might have pushed the kid out twenty-five years before—there was no denying that, to look at Joelle's face—but Callie never played house with her. And still the girl managed to follow in her footsteps. The stupid bitch. No surprise there though, she even had the balls to show up and claim the relation. As if it got her anything on the inside.

Normally, Callie ignored her each time she made any reference to it. Reacting only encouraged her more. Not this time, though.

"Any maternal instincts I had died a long time ago, chicky, right about the time my milk of human kindness dried up. You would do well to keep that in mind. You are nothing to me but a punk stupid enough to try and challenge me."

Wisely, Joelle remained silent. Callie waved her on to the Mess but lingered behind herself. She took a quickl glance back down the corridor. The door to the Yard was still open as the last of the guards entered the building. Past their shoulders, she could just make out the Feds hustling their prisoner to Processing. There were two chain-link fences, with great rolls of razor wire coiled at the base of each one, and the dead zone between them, but it was like none of that was there, as if no more than a few feet were between them. Two things she noticed immediately: this one was big and tall... like Guinness World Record tall, and for some reason she was wrapped in an odd, layered cloak that looked like soft, buttery leather.

Callie took in the rest of the woman, weighing what she saw. The matte black hair wafting down her back swayed as if ruffled by a breeze, though the air was dead still, and below the cloak the woman's calves and feet were bare. Perhaps the prison system hadn't had anything large enough to cover them. Or perhaps the behemoth had a nasty disposition to go with that imposing physique and no one dare get close enough to outfit her properly. She was shackled, though, hand and foot. The links were made of steel thick enough that Callie could make them out clearly from where she stood.

Things were about to get interesting.

The new prisoner stopped, forcing the Feds in front to scramble back. They yelled and menaced the prisoner, trying to get her to resume moving forward. To Callie, they seemed like teeny-tiny Chihuahuas snapping at the legs of a Great Dane. The Great Dane ignored them; instead she turned and looked back. Their eyes met. Callie longed to jerk hers away, but the woman's tar-black gaze was inescapable.

Across the distance, the prisoner's head tilted ever so slightly, as if she were listening for something. Her face was both disturbingly devoid of expression and fierce all at once. Her eyes were sharp and assessing, so overt it was grounds for a slap-down on the Block. Callie lifted her chin and allowed her lip to curl. She dared the woman to judge her. So she was big, and whatever she had done, it had both the Feds and the guards as worked up as a prairie dog town with ferret musk on the air, but Callie backed down to no one.

The prisoner nodded, and then turned and walked from sight, followed by the startled Feds, their procession in total disarray.

The mess hall was thick with whispers.

"No prison will have her..."

"...people end up dead..."

"They say she's a monster."

Callie ignored the gossip. Wasn't no one in this place—inmate or guard—what wasn't a monster in some way, and people were always dying... with or without help. She wasn't going to give credence to any talk. If this new one wanted a face-down, Callie would put her in her place; if not, she wasn't worth the speculation. None of them were.

She gathered her tray and the slop they were dishing and turned to her usual spot: A table along the back wall where she could see everything, and no one could come at her back. The table was large, heavy, industrial grade, and supposedly bolted to the floor. Over the years, Callie had removed and stripped those bolts, using any tool she could get her hands on to cut off most of the length until only a nub was left to hold the bolt in the hole. When she'd done it, it had mostly been a matter of boredom, and wanting to rebel against the establishment. Besides, tipped over, the table would make a good shield, or even a diversion, if she needed one. The table was hers, an indication of her power.

Some people didn't get that... or maybe they did.

Joelle was already there, sitting in Callie's seat. That girl had to push it; and several other dumb fucks had joined her.

Callie had no problem pushing back. She slid a look to the others at the table, her gaze snapping and her expression deadly flat. Most of them immediately swept up their lunches and cleared away. A couple of the dumber ones hesitated, as if feeling for a shift in power. Callie just smiled and let her breath out in a soft *hmph*. She half closed her lids, looking them each in the eye. Without a word, but with plenty of haste, they abandoned their trays and scurried to other tables.

Once she and Joelle had a measure of privacy, Callie braced her hands on the edges of the tabletop, taking a good grip, her legs braced and her stance wide.

"Perhaps you didn't believe me earlier," she spoke, her eyes as hard as her voice was soft.

Furtive glances shot their way an instant before they were conscientiously ignored. Around them, the conversations climbed several decibels, giving them a bit of cover, of sorts.

It was good to be the Queen. Or the Alpha bitch, anyway. Callie intended to stay in power, and took the necessary steps to strengthen her position.

"You know, you had yourself a baby brother for a while." Callie leaned forward keeping her tone low, so Joelle had to strain to catch her words. "One night I woke up and watched as my man smothered the squalling brat, when he was done I snuck up and killed him before he could do the same to me."

She watched as her careful words formed the proper picture in the space behind Joelle's eyes, watched as they summoned Callie's earlier words: no maternal instinct, no milk of human kindness. The girl went pale and then green, then her lip curled in revulsion. Fear, however, was absent from her gaze.

The fool still did not get it.

Callie shot a look to the side and caught a loyal eye. She jerked her head toward the far side of the room. Moments later, a fight broken out and distracted the guards.

"I believe in taking care of my problems before they take care of me," Callie purred, as she turned her full attention back to Joelle. The girl tensed and looked to either side. More inmates loyal to Callie had drifted in the spaces to either side of the table. Though seemingly not paying attention, they blocked any way of escape.

With a nasty smirk and a massive heave, Callie yanked up hard on the table, popping the bolts out of their holes. Trays clattered to the floor. Joelle gasped. She might have yelled, except Callie rammed the table hard into her chest. There was a thud and a crack, splintering wood from the chair echoed sharply by shattering bone. Joelle glared, teeth clenched against the pain and hatred and defiance barely masked. She hid the fear better, but Callie caught the tremor ripping beneath the dumb bitch's skin. For good measure, Callie yanked the table back and slammed it home again. Then she leaned heavy into the edge and ground it from side to side until it crushed the younger woman a little more.

Joelle gave a strangled gasp, but clearly did not have the air to scream. Her eyes went wide and glassy. Callie ran her gaze appraisingly over her daughter and let a sneer just barely peak her lip. This one was too stupid to live. She could see Joelle's hatred break loose and blossom full in her expression. The girl would have spit if Callie had let up on the steady pressure of the table. She bucked weakly and Callie shoved harder, until blood trickled from the girl's mouth and her eyes turned to hard, lifeless pebbles.

Callie yanked the table back into place and Joelle's body slid silently beneath. Thanks to those loyal to her, none of the guards noticed the goings on. Eventually, someone would say something, but what were they going to do, incarcerate her in the next life too? As long as they did not find the body too soon, any accusations would only be allegations, anyway. Callie kicked the trays on the floor beneath the table with the rest of the trash, and then moved off across the room, the picture of innocence.

It was then that she heard a whisper out of nowhere, drifting on the stale, greasy air of the mess hall. "The sins of the mother… blood calls for blood."

She shrugged it off and turned her back on Joelle. The girl was in no position to attack, and Callie's supremacy remained unchallenged.

Lock Down came early. Callie lay in her cot as the guards shut the Block down for the night. She was too wired to sleep.

Joelle had been discovered at the end of lunch, during head count, as the guards were divvying the inmates up into their work crews. The uproar had been exhilarating, the wrath of the establishment tempered by an taut edge of fear Callie could not explain, unless it had to do with the newbie and the things everyone whispered about her. Satisfaction pulled Callie's lips into a seldom-used smile.

Unless someone talked, it didn't seem Callie would ever come under suspicion. She was home free; she'd already made it clear what would happen if anyone said a thing.

She could not sleep. She lay there waiting for dawn to come, her mind buzzing and her body tense with the need to move and do something.

There was a whimper in the semi-darkness, like that of a baby, then a miserable cry. Callie sat up, startled, her pulse racing for some reason she could not explain. She tried to tell herself it was just the excitement of the day working on her nerves, but even as she thought it, the cry escalated into a scream, cut off... smothered by the silence. No one on the Block reacted, not inmate or guard. It was as if the scream had sounded only for Callie's ears.

Suddenly, she could not breathe. She thrashed, slammed her fists into the thin mattress. She felt the weight of the shadows like a pillow over her face, heavier and heavier, anchored by memories... memories of her boy, and of her man. Good memories and bad. Fatal memories. Memories of her daughter. Callie pushed them all away. Her heart hardened. Her face twisted with rage. They meant nothing to her. She stopped being soft long before they drew their last breathes.

Callie forced air into her petrified lungs and unclenched her muscles. With a thought, she cut off the memories. Breathing did not get any easier.

Silence, heavy, thick, and suffocating. Callie fought against it with each breath. She opened her eyes to a shape looming above her, somehow within her cell. The woman's head practically brushed the twelve-foot ceiling. And, with a *whoosh*, her wings filled the cell.

Callie fought not to cringe, not to strain her eyes to make out the figure before her. It was the newbie, no question. Who else was that big?

Wings? Callie's eyes went wide, the faint light from the corridor backlighting the impossible and imposing wings. "What are you doing here?" she demanded, not even wondering how the bitch broke free of wherever she was being held and ended up in Callie's cell.

"Taking care of business."

"Business? The only business we have in here is to rot." Callie sneered, hiding her growing terror behind toughness.

"No. Your business is to pay."

In an instant, the memories flooded back. Boy babies and girl babies... bruises and needles and punches upside the head... screams... and whimpers... and telling silences. Callie moaned and clenched her fists. She tried to force the memories away once more. Her hands came up to cover her ears and she curled around herself like a baby in the womb. The weight of the world landed on her chest, or at least twelve, tall feet of it did, slamming her flat into the cot, not letting her hide. She looked up into that terrible face. One she had no problem seeing, despite the low light. It was her own face, aside from the eyes. Black, depthless eyes that saw everything with an unforgiving clarity.

Callie gulped and thrashed. Or at least she tried to. That face came closer. The hair framing it caressed her cheek. It did not feel like hair. It did not move like hair. Tiny slivers of fire pierced Callie's skin all over her face and neck. She could feel venom creeping through her veins. Her ears filled with a furious hissing, low and inescapable. No, it did not move like hair. It moved like snakes.

"You... in this place... because you're a monster?"

"No, because you are. Time to pay."

The words were somehow soft and hard and vibrant all at once, the epitome of fury. Callie whimpered. Tears mingled with the blood running in tiny tendrils down her face. She tried to bring her hands up, to push her tormentor away. She could not move, and she could not close her eyes. Her gaze was riveted, but she no longer saw the Fury perched on her chest.

The memories came flooding back.

"Save... me," Callie begged to die long before she finally did.

KYLIE'S SCREAMS SHREDDED THE AIR THE WAY SHARDS OF GLASS cut through cobwebs. She jerked back, her hands shaking violently. Something cool and slimy flew off them and slapped against Don's cheek as he brought his hands up to steady her.

"Eww! Eww! EWWW!"

He didn't say a word, but Don agreed; whatever she'd flicked off her hand had slid down his face and was now heading inside his shirt. He lifted one hand off Kylie's shoulder to intercept it. His fingers rubbed across something the consistency of chilled jelly. Every year the haunted house changed. Whoever designed it this year had gone all-out.

The effort was not lost on his baby sister.

"No! No! I can't do it! I can't! I want to go back," Kylie whimpered. She continued to back up until she pressed tight against his chest. When he didn't move, she slammed herself into him and pushed, as if determination alone would send him the way they had come. Somewhere in the dark ahead of them rose a witch's cackle. Kylie jumped at the sudden sound and renewed her efforts with more force. Her little body crashed against him like a battering ram. He had to brace himself more than once as she pulled away and slammed back over and over. For all her fierceness, he smelled the acrid scent of her fear and responded.

"Shhh... shhhh..." With ten years between their ages, Don was used to soothing his twelve-year-old sister. They shared some link that made him particularly suited for it, a connection beyond the norm. He couldn't explain except to call it a mental ability. Not telepathy, not empathy, but something that allowed him to influence her. He could not *make* her do things, but if emotion clouded reason, he could clear it away, kind of like calming by osmosis. It worked best if they were touching, but that was not necessary.

His clean hand came off her shoulder and smoothed her sandy curls so he could rest his chin on top of her head. As he did so, he brought both arms around her slender shoulders in a sheltering hug. He spoke because she expected it, though it was not what he said out loud that made a difference. "Come on, darlin'. It's OK. We're almost there."

"I want to go back." This time she braced against him and used her muscular legs to push him back. "I *want* to go back!"

Kylie was nothing if not stubborn. He could hear it in her voice. Intractable, unyielding... she would dig in with both feet all night. Leaning forward to cancel out her nearly successful efforts, he chuckled and rubbed her arms gently.

"Sweetie," Don allowed amusement to edge into his voice. "Think about it—we're over halfway through. If we turn around now, you'll just have to go by the creepy stuff all over again."

She remained silent for a long moment. He could feel her scalp shift forward. In his mind, he saw the glowering pout so familiar to him. He gave her a little extra squeeze, another mental push. Growling, she slapped at his arms until he let her go.

"Never again! *Never* again, Donkey-breath!" She whirled as she spit the words at him. As she turned, artificial lightning cracked through the dank "graveyard" they stood in the middle of. The setting and the spooky glow made her glare downright ghoulish despite the silver tracks of tears glittering on her cheeks. If she weren't so young and his kid sister, Don would have been doing some serious backpedaling himself. Instead, he smiled.

"Come on, Ky, you say that every year. This was *your* idea, you know."

Her scowl deepened and her hands curled into hard little fists. He chuckled and grabbed them before she could bring them into play.

"Hey, find the way out and the caramel apple's on me."

Her fists stayed clenched, but the scowl lost all its heat. Kylie suddenly grinned as if she were six.

"A caramel apple *and* cotton candy," she countered.

Don let go of her hands, held out one of his own, and shook on it. He chuckled and waited patiently as she visibly gathered her courage to move forward. They weren't in any rush. The lady who tore their tickets told them they were the last ones for the night, so it wasn't like anyone was going to come upon them.

Ahead, the shrieks and laughter of those who had gone before grew fainter. Time to continue on or they would end up locked in for the night. They moved through darkness and shadow in a quick hustle. Canned shrieks and maniacal laughter kept pace with them while burning red "eyes" blinked from unexpected places. The occasional denizens of the dungeon leapt out, only to fade back once Kylie screamed. Near the end, the floor beneath the grate they walked on fell away to reveal the illusion of a raging inferno below, as if they were about to plummet straight to hell. Kylie simply clutched his hand a little tighter and plowed through, squealing as low flying "bats" zipped by.

Finally, the moss-draped exit came into sight. Don barely registered Kylie's gasp as the door clanged shut behind them. He was too busy gulping hard. The exit had not led outside; it led to a hall of mirrors.

He turned to push back through into the haunted house, only to find that there were no handles on this side of the door.

"Wow..." Kylie's tone came out hushed with awe. The wonder in her voice drew him back around. He struggled to force down his own less-eager reaction. For her, Don plastered a smile on his face. A strained grimace reflected back at him a thousand-fold.

Crap. This was not good. If he'd known this was here, he would have given in to Kylie's insistence to go back the other way. Something lurked behind the silver-backed glass, something hungry. Something primal instinct told him to avoid. He'd encountered it once as a child and had avoided mirrored mazes ever since. Hell, he avoided any mirror, if he could.

This time he had no choice; the way out led straight through that perilous maze. For the first time ever, Don wished his link with Kylie went both ways. The best she could do was hold his hand, but his ego could not stand the blow of letting her know how freaked out he was.

"Oh, wow! Will you get a load of this..." Kylie started forward and it was Don's turn to dig in his heels. She turned to look at him, the memory of her own fear quickly fading. The corners of her mouth drew down and her brow furrowed as she grabbed his hand and tugged.

"Come on, Don Quixote, face your demons."

Internally, Don flinched. Demons. Apt word. Thousands upon thousands of them stared back at him. Each one wore his face. Literally mirroring his every move. In theory, he held power over them. After all, what could a reflection do but follow his steps? His forehead immediately filmed over with sweat. He gave in to his need to keep hold of her hand. He had learned long ago that reflections could be more than they seemed.

"Cut it out, Ky."

"Hey, it's just a maze." Her tone softened as she saw through his efforts to remain calm. "Let's go; we'll be through it in no time. I promise, this time I'll protect *you*."

Reluctantly, he let her draw him forward. He watched the thing with his face, waited for it to make its move. When he looked at it head-on, it matched him exactly, over and over in endless repetition. Except for the glimpses he caught from the corner of his eye. Those made him tense. Those expressions and actions did not exactly mirror Don's own.

He continued to let Kylie lead the way. Her reflection stayed true to form, never deviating. She came up against the mirrors and merely pushed away, continuing her search for the pathway out. That was how it should be. The natural order of things.

Don meticulously avoided the walls of the maze.

Kylie laughed and the sound tinkled off the glass. Hard to believe no less than ten minutes ago she'd been petrified. Don clutched her hand tighter. Without realizing it, his steps slowed. Their arms stretched between them. In the mirrors, his reflection reached for him. His eyes went wide, and he shuddered to a stop.

"Whoa... hello! My arm is attached," Kylie groused. "I'd kinda like it to stay that way. Come on, it's not funny anymore. What's up with you, anyway?"

He could not answer. She gave a tug and he followed. They left the corridor and found themselves in a huge, octagonal chamber with enough space to hold a small dance. The center of the maze.

As they stepped fully into the room, a sharp click sounded. The lights dimmed even further as the floor slowly rose and tilted like a low, wide top. Another click and a disco ball lowered from the ceiling. The spangled light effect combined with the shifting floor disoriented Don.

Kylie giggled and pulled him into the center of the room. The floor continued to tilt, but not enough to make them fall. She grabbed him by both hands and with a mischievous grin she started them spinning. Her laughter rose bright and good. Don's terror ebbed and he told himself not to be silly. The nightmares he had had since childhood were not possible. What he half-remembered from that long-ago time in another hall of mirrors could not be possible.

His sister's joy and his own common sense chased back the demons. He smiled and put effort into spinning them even faster, leaning back, as Kylie did, to increase their momentum. The disco ball picked up speed, the floor tipped steeper. Don added his laughter to his sister's. The faster they went, the more their fingers slipped from each other's grip.

"Oh, shit!" Don reached frantically to strengthen his hold. What were they thinking? He had visions of them flying backward into the glass. Images of shattered, bloody shards flashed in his mind.

"No!"

He could not help it. His grip released and they both flew back in opposite directions, Kylie laughing all the way. She was still laughing when they landed. No tinkle of shattered glass followed.

Don hit hard, but not against the mirrored wall, though even with his eyes closed he could tell it was close. For a moment he could not move. When he could, it was only to roll onto his stomach. His body shook in delayed reaction and, in his thoughts, Don thanked the Lord that their stupidity had not had worse consequences. He rested his forehead on the ground and called out to his sister.

"Hey, Ky... you OK?"

"Yeah." Giggles threaded her voice, and he heard the faint scraping of denim as she picked herself up.

"How about you?"

"Just give me a minute."

Bracing both arms against the floor, Don looked up to see just how close he had come to disaster. He gulped as his hair brushed the wall. He blinked, eyes rising to the mirror. His dazed surface reflection stared back. Something else gleamed beneath it. Fear flooded to the fore. He scrambled to his feet too quickly. His heart clenched hard and he could not get a breath. He swayed and felt himself fall forward.

The mirror was too close. His choices were to brace against the glass or fall into it. Before he could decide, his hand came up in automatic reflex. Rested against the cool surface, it stabilized his balance in that critical moment. He blinked his eyes and drew a hard breath. Any second he expected his world to end. Nothing happened.

He laughed and the sound had an edge to it. What a complete spaz, letting a silly childhood fear tie him into knots. His forehead came to rest against the mirror. His eyes drifted closed. A moment to relax, to regain his equilibrium, that's all he needed.

That moment was all his reflection needed, as well.

A sharp tingle burned across his skin. Eyes snapping open, Don stared into his nightmares. The gaze that met his own in the mirror gleamed black with hatred, thick with jealousy. Venom whispered through his thoughts. It reminded him of his link with Kylie, only twisted.

'Hello, brother.'

What the hell! The thought formed, but Don knew he did not voice it out loud. That did not seem to make a difference. He struggled to pull back, to break contact, but the mirror held him fast, as if his flesh had melded with the glass.

'You've been avoiding me. Time to get a little closer...'

Don had no chance to respond. A shock raced over his skin. Then a second one, deeper still. His body buzzed. He throbbed and ached with the sensation. It felt like two of him fought to occupy his skin. The world darkened and dimmed around him. He tried to scream. It sounded only in the silence of his mind.

What are you? He forced the thought past the pain.

'*Why, I'm your evil twin.*'

Don put every ounce of effort into pulling away. Agony ripped at him. A malicious chuckle tore through his mind as some force yanked him forward. He fought it with everything he had.

'*Behave, brother, it's my turn to come out and play.*'

You bastard!

'*Actually, I prefer Skippy.*'

Faint and far off, a sound drew Don's attention from the struggle. His heart clenched and a moan shuddered through him.

"Don, you okay?"

No! Kylie! But he could not answer. The demon had silenced him. It took everything he had to fight back.

"Hey, Don Juan, you're scaring me here. You hit your head or something? Or are you just busy making kissy-face with your reflection?"

An evil laugh drowned out whatever else she might have said. Don shrieked as a surge of power washed over him. Intense pain... a tingle across his skin. He fell, his body passing through endless slivers of glass.

He landed hard. There was nothing left but agony and bright light. He forced his way past the torment. Scrambling to his feet, he turned and sought his sister. Panic nearly threw him down again. He saw her through a smoky haze, from every possible angle at once. Already disoriented, Don swayed. He closed his eyes against the sensation. Silence and darkness wrapped him tight. He stood stranded in a vacuum with Kylie trapped outside.

Don's eyes flew open again and he fought to focus through just one view, to be in a single place at once. He stared into Kylie's face, but her gaze did not quite meet his. She smiled at the Don-who-was-not-Don as if nothing had changed. The love and trust in her gaze were tangible as she reached for his hand. For *Skippy's* hand.

No! Ky... Ky! Don frantically tried to make her hear him. *Sweetie, run! That's not me!* His voice cracked and he pounded on the haze, desperate to shatter it. He fell.

Laughter sounded again in his head, in sharp, shredding jags.

'There's nothing there for you to hit, dear brother—not unless I touch it from this side.'

Skippy's malice rode the twisted link and hit Don hard. In reaction, rage shook him. He ground his teeth against another scream. He would not give the demon more cause to taunt him. Don's focus slipped and he saw his nightmare from a thousand dizzying views. Ky and Skippy moved off, heading for the second half of the maze. Determined, Don followed them.

His every step mirrored Skippy's. At first, he fought it, but the drain ate away at him. It stole his thoughts and his will until he could not remember why he fought at all. He was too new to the mirror realm to fight it. That added to Don's fury. Skippy's motions forced Don to follow, to watch, helpless as Kylie scrambled to keep up. The demon ruthlessly dragged her through the maze.

Don gave up on calling out to his sister. The place that trapped him also hedged in his words. Gritting his teeth, he locked his eyes on Kylie. He had to reach her. He thought of the link they shared, tried to sense if it still remained. The effort nearly floored him; would have, if he were not chained to Skippy's motions. His will struggled as if he were encased in thick glass. The mirror realm muffled everything, including the link between him and his sister. He could tell it remained, but only as a mere shadow of itself. He called it. Willed all of his strength into it. Did something he had never done before: used it to make his sister anything but calm. He projected an image at her, one where she fought the grip of a stranger masked by Don's face. He felt, more than saw, as doubt and uncertainty took hold of her. Beginning wisps of fear drifted into her gaze. She no longer scurried to keep up.

Skippy shot Don a venomous look through the mirror's reflection but did not speak or slow his pace. If anything, his steps grew more urgent. Don roared and whipped his fist through the haze. He knew now what drove his evil twin: the exit. They were nearly out. And once they passed the threshold Don would lose his chance of escape.

'Yes! Yes, you will.' Skippy hissed in Don's thoughts. *'Once we go through, you are damned forever... trapped forever.'*

Insanity tinged the demon's laughter. From the look on Kylie's face, she had heard it as well. She stumbled and Skippy jerked her hard to her feet, not even stopping.

Don thought the image at her again, stirring her doubt. He wavered with the effort.

Kylie instantly transformed. Her fear and confusion morphed into a familiar glower. Her free hand fisted and her feet planted firm and would not be budged.

Yes! Don knew his first glimmer of hope since he had been yanked through the glass.

Come on, honey, come on. Look at him, Kylie. See *him!* That could never be me.

Get away, Ky!

He watched as her gaze went from Skippy, to his reflection, and back again. She could not possibly hear Don, or see him, but did she begin to consciously feel him? Her brow drew down even further and she showed her teeth.

Yes!

That's it. You wouldn't take any of that from me... don't take it from him, Kylie. I love you, sweetie. Just get away.

Don gathered all his will and focused everything on the thought of his sister getting free, pictured her pulling away. His frustration built as Skippy dragged Kylie closer to the exit. One of the demon's hands reached for the handle, while his other jerked Kylie brutally, drawing her along.

Kylie growled and yanked back but could not break Skippy's grip. Don watched her yank again, throwing all of her body behind the effort. He continued his pinpoint focus on her, trying to lend her strength. He weakened and his world went several shades darker. He hardly noticed as Kylie slammed backward, dragging her hand from Skippy's. She collided with one of the mirrored panels. A spider's web of cracks fractured the silver-backed surface, the impact point smudged with blood; Kylie slid to the floor. She did not move.

Don cried out and tried to go to her, but he could find no way through the haze. His rage built and he no longer feared the demon. Not when he meant to tear it apart.

He looked up and met Skippy's gaze. As earlier, his reflection showed him fear. This time not his own.

'*No! You cannot touch me!*' Skippy screamed in Don's mind. '*You cannot pass back. It's* my *turn!*'

Don just stared at him, as if memorizing a face he'd not seen before. He allowed his intentions to shine through. Skippy paled and backed away. Don just smiled an unpleasant smile. He also noticed something he had missed: the haze around him slowly thinned, like smoke escaping through a crack. Sound filtered through the fractured mirror—calliope music, the hawkers' last cries from beyond the exit door, and Kylie's moan, as she came back to herself.

The smile on Don's face took on a satisfied gleam. The moment he heard his sister's unmuffled moan, he knew. Mentally, he reached out to her and his suspicions were confirmed: The barrier was breached. The horror on Skippy's face clinched it. Don reached up and placed his hand against the haze, watched it shimmer and deepen to a silver sheen. Skippy scrambled back, colliding with a mirror on the other side.

This time Don purposely eased back his focus. He went from the singular point he'd clung to, to being everywhere at once. The tightness returned as Don stared into the madness of Skippy's haunted eyes. With a thought, he drew the demon to him with an unyielding grip. Again, Don's body held two of him. No agony, this time, but as he pushed through what felt like a stream of warm silk, he heard Skippy's tortured scream as the other fell back through endless slivers of glass.

Don landed hard with his senses still cloaked in a shimmery haze. Avoiding the glass, he pushed himself off the floor. He knelt in place, legs spread wide until he swayed no more. He raised his eyes to his reflection, braced for a glimpse of Skippy's hatred.

The mirror held nothing of the other. Don's reflection stared back at him from the glass, and it was him alone. Skippy was gone.

Only then did Don edge forward. He pulled Kylie into his lap and wrapped his arms around her. She stirred as he pressed his lips to the top of her head.

"Welcome back," she murmured, her voice faint as she sank into his hug. "Where'd you go?"

Don smiled down at her and whispered back, "You don't want to know, but for busting me out, you get *two* caramel apples."

RUBY RED

THERE WAS BLOOD ON THE COUNTER. JUST THREE LITTLE DROPS, bright and deep all at once. Startling against the white marble. I ran my finger through one gleaming half-globe. It smeared a red spectrum along the edge of the sink.

I giggled. The sound startled me. It was out of place in the surrounding starkness, slashing a hole in the silence that closed instantly. I was being disrespectful.

Dragging my lower lip between my teeth, I reached for the roll of tissue and tore off a couple of squares. With great care, I wiped away the smear I'd made, leaving the remaining two drops pristine and the rest of the counter nothing but white. I balled the tissue and clutched it tight in my fist.

The urge to giggle swept through me once more, and I ground down harder on my lip. The pain was sharp and focusing. It allowed me to fight back the urge. It had been so long since I'd been allowed color. They didn't trust me with color. Things happened.

I wrapped my arms tight around my body and stared at the remaining two drops. Lost myself in the play of light upon the gleaming surfaces. They sparkled like gems. My breath quickened, and I had to tuck my hands beneath my arms to keep them still, to keep them from reaching out and playing with the pretty color.

"Red," I whispered. It was no more than a breath, nearly just a thought. I didn't want anyone to hear. They would take the drops away. "Red... red like rubies, like poppies under the sun, strawberries dripping with dew."

The intensity ran like a wire up my spine. Each word drew it taut; each image sprang into my mind and spawned more. I buried my senses in each thing that surfaced. My eyes were dazzled by the glimmer of jewels, my nose filled with the smell of warm flowers, my tongue savored the sweetness of ripe fruit.

"Red!"

The bathroom became a sea of red as my mental images shaped reality. Flower petals scattered over the cold, white tile; ripe fruit crushed beneath my feet as I circled the room. Power swirled around me, brushed my skin, danced among the strands of my hair. It was red as well. Everything was red.

I laughed with the joy of color. The white was swept away. Bending, I scooped my hands through the redness and encountered sharp-edged gems. I'd found my rubies. The sting of pain was life and I laughed more. Gone was the sterile white. I lifted my arms, pale, white skin trailing beads of blood from a hundred little nicks.

"Red! Red like blood!"

The bite of iron overwhelmed my other senses: the smell, the taste, the slick, thick feel of it against my skin. A liquid red tide swept over me, coating the walls and sweeping away fruit and flowers and gems.

"Red... red like blood," I whispered again, a mere moving of the lips, drowned out by the pulse of the tide.

Red swept me away.

WHITE. THE DRESS WAS BLINDING WHITE, SETTING OFF THE DARK, burnished-gold curls that fell to her shoulders in a simple pony tail, so innocent in an age of decadence. I'd never been close enough to see her eyes, though I knew they were light, and supposed they were cornflower blue, as I expected most blondes to be.

But ever since the first day I saw her, she drew me like a lodestone. Without thought or fail, I repeatedly found myself here, across from where she lived. We never spoke, but I could not help but watch over her from time to time. There was no question that I was unworthy. I did not even know her name, but her face was engraved on my heart. Yet still, I kept my distance, content to love the image of her, or so I told myself, for it was all I could ever hope to have.

Apart from her, I occasionally dreamed of the life we'd have together if I had the right to pursue one. I imagined the love and joy and warmth long denied me. The laughter of children and the comfort of a passing caress. I would see her in the morning light and feel her beside me... in my arms... as I drifted off at night.

In her presence, I found myself obsessed and every day worked hard to keep away, fought to close off the darker imaginings, the fantasies of perverted pleasures that surfaced each time I saw her. I was not myself. Never before had I been enticed by such depravity. Quite the opposite—it disgusted me in others. To begin now, with an object of such clear innocence, shamed me... thrilled me.

No!

Today she drew nearer than ever before; as close as the width of the street, strolling down the opposite sidewalk toward the harbor as if without care, the handles of a half-filled plastic bag twined about her wrist, looking oddly provocative. The street around her seemed to suffer in contrast, appearing shabbier, more corrupted by decay. In her wake the worst of humanity seemed to spring. Conversations transformed into fights, well-behaved children became shades of Damian; even normally docile pets seemed to grow vicious, as if her perfection reflected badly upon the rest of the world. But then, I did not doubt that anything and anyone would suffer in comparison to her. Such was her flawlessness that I expected to hear the songs of cherubim and seraphim as she passed.

Instead, the wind whispered, "Come..." in the quiet voice of a solitary angel. "Come along..." it whispered again.

I scarcely needed persuading in the face of such temptation.

I will not approach her, I swore to myself. *I'll only see her safely wherever she is bound.* I allowed myself to follow behind and my mind again dwelt on things that had nothing to do with innocence as I watched the sway of her long white skirt.

As she drew close to the harbor—turning in, rather than passing by as I expected— wisps of unease filled my heart until I crept closer than I'd intended. As with everything else, she was a jarring contrast to the rude nature of the docks. What was she doing here? It was not a safe place to wander as ships disgorged floods of heavy cargo and long-isolated men. What if I were not here to look after her? I shuddered at the possibilities my mind easily supplied—dark thoughts already hidden in the recesses of my soul. An unexpected growl rumbled in my chest and I flexed my hands to keep them from fisting for no reason but my imaginings.

Dock workers and sailors, working with tight focus and steady diligence as she approached, fell away from their tasks to stare as she went by. I watched their faces and my chest tightened at the transformation. Hunger flooded their eyes, one and all. Violence rose in some. None turned away once she moved on. A few even set aside their burdens and followed in her wake, sharing glances among them, which I did not care for in the least. The beginnings of anger bubbled up from my depths. I recognized a danger different from the ones I feared before.

The men called out as they drew closer, a vulgar mockery of the heavenly host I'd expected earlier. My beauty ignored them. Moving to the end of the dock, she drew some Italian bread from her sack. She held the narrow loaf in both hands, again... innocently provocative. I fought myself as readily as I prepared to fight the other men. I fought not to imagine her grip stroking up and down the hard length, fought not to imagine it was me cradled in her hands. My stomach soured with the shock of my thoughts. I barely won my battle as she watched the sky, waiting for the gulls to gather.

The birds came... and so did the vultures.

My jaw clenched, followed by my fists. I slid closer to the woman and turned until the denizens of the docks could not look upon her without seeing me... and the dire purpose in my expression. They ignored the warning.

"Whoa, babe, you can haul my anchor any time."

More of the same was bandied about, growing progressively cruder, and subtly more threatening. Each taunt was punctuated by laughter and ravenous glances. I growled deep in my throat. An uncharacteristic rage rapidly filled my heart. For the first time that day I was blind to the innocent beauty I'd trailed to the harbor. Was blind, in fact, to all around me but the men I was intent on turning away.

"You need to get back to work, and leave the lady alone." I kept my tone low and even and my body poised.

They laughed at me, looking to one another and then back to my lone self. Their lewd leers grew calculating, as hard and dangerous as my own must have been. The tools of their trade were brought forth; powerful, meaty hands drew out baling knives and cargo hooks, others swept up flotsam that littered the dock, one just grinned viciously, bounced with a sailor's balance, and gleefully balled his fists.

A gasp from behind nearly distracted me as the men drew their circle tighter. A feather-light touch on my shoulder succeeded. My skin ignited beneath her fingers, ran like a fuse straight to my groin. My gaze snapped back to meet hers and I was trapped by the concern in her eyes, the tension subtly evident in her expression. With each degree that she paled I felt myself darken in rage.

Mine! My inner beast screamed. *Mine! Not theirs!*

Her startled and fearful face was the last thing I saw as reality fell in upon me, borne upon the fists of dangerous men. I echoed her screams as agony sliced through my gut. Before I could turn away, darkness claimed me.

I fought the pain to open my eyes. Perfection hovered over me. The faint wail of sirens filtered to my ears. Some satisfaction crept into my heart. We were alone and I could see no sign of harm upon her.

I could not say the same for me.

My throat spasmed and the stench of blood and death came to me upon my own breath. She gasped as I stared up at her, fighting to focus on her face. I would have gasped myself, had I been able. With clarity I'd lacked before these final moments I saw the truth of my innocent beauty. I saw the miasma previously hidden to me. She was a bright, hot flame surrounded by dark vapors. What could only be evil seeped from her pores and rode her breath, odorless and deadly. It settled upon me one last time, and I struggled not to breathe it in.

The lovely one's eyes were steeped in horror and distress. Her eyes were not cornflower blue, but bright, startling green like the back of a frog from the Brazilian rainforest—beautiful, but poisonous. They held a whisper of my pain as compassion swept her along with me. I looked away from those kind, yet monstrous eyes, unable to bear the insidious truth: somehow they remained pure and devoid of deceit. Even knowing what I did, she was yet the picture of innocence. My dimming gaze trailed down her sundress, captured by the deep red stain marring the virginal white. I suddenly wanted to laugh; the innocence lost was my own, as was the blood.

Again, I was distracted as the softest of caresses graced my brow, like those I'd long dreamed about between us. With that touch, despair filled my heart. I fought the clenching of my throat and forced myself to again look into her eyes. All color faded from the world, but I could imagine the green of her gaze was still there.

"Who... are you?" I breathed out a bare whisper.

She tried to smile through her anguish. Leaning down over me, her eyes bright with verging tears, her blood-stained breast pressed flush against me as she brushed her lips across my ear. She uttered one word, "Angel." Her voice low and husky with emotion, sounding almost sultry, so at odds with the vision of innocence I'd thought her to be. I wondered which part of what I'd seen was a delusion, the product of my fading. My fear.

She pulled back just enough that we were face to face. The threatening tears poured down her cheeks, glittering like diamonds on porcelain. Her eyes definitely flared emerald green into my black-and-white reality, but only a moment before she placed her lips upon mine in a chaste kiss then slowly, carefully pulled back, drawing away with her my soul.

The Forest of a Thousand Lost Souls

A GOOD GENERAL DOES NOT ALLOW THE ENEMY TO SELECT THE FIELD of battle. I am thought by others to be the best. I should have tried much harder...

I.

It was autumn as my troops gathered on the field at Asculus, a barren plain wedged between the mountains and the sea. Surrounding valleys bore the bristled signs of a successful harvest; our current training ground had seen so much blood spilt in its long history as to never be free of the resulting sown salt. In the summer's heat, the scent still rose from the soil, rousingly speaking to us of battle. It was permanently marked for the business of war. And for that, we prepared.

The Enemy threatened from the Savage Lands. Our emperor summoned his forces. We were not the only soldiers to assemble, but we were his chosen. We would lead the fray. Each day, proud young faces filled out our ranks and, for me, the sun lost that much more of its brilliance with each one. I did not allow myself to wonder who would fall in the battles to come; instead, I dedicated myself to honing them into a lethal force. They must follow my lead without question, for I knew I would see the next harvest, and many more to come; the same could not necessarily be said for them. There was no doubt I would burn more than a third of my forces on assorted pyres before the planted fields were once again ripe, and that only if I were lucky. I expected it to be more.

What melancholy had crept into my heart? I mourned my dead too soon and did not do justice to my men. Yet how could it be otherwise? In the darkest hours of night, I was tormented by the knowledge that I led so many young men to their deaths. I have been an officer a very long time.

I forced the darkness from me. Climbing the wooden dais, I moved to the spot left open for me, standing shoulder to shoulder with my captains. Silence descended.

"Who are you?" I challenged them, as I have countless troops before.

"General, we are the Emperor's Elite!" Their voices rose in precise unison and I allowed myself a moment of pride. These warriors would serve the emperor well. The strength of their response flooded me, charging the blood in my veins with added vigor. It made me confidant that we were invincible, my earlier doubts banished.

"And how shall you fight?" I continued, keeping my tone outwardly neutral.

"We will fight with His might... We will fight with His valor... Our courage is His."

I paused, waiting a beat before continuing, allowing them to settle down from their fervor.

"Your emperor has summoned you to war and I am here to see that you are ready to vanquish our enemy. Your first lesson: Forget the songs you have heard sung of glorious battle. Heroes are not made in war, but created after, by those who have no concept of its horror." Their faces lifted up to me, filled with awe. My men marveled at the strength of my words. Little did they know, as much as I spoke to them, I spoke more to myself. "Look to the men before and to either side of you... turn and seek the faces of those at your back... these are your brothers, and as they stand beside you, so you stand beside them.

"Do not forget this: the praise or damnation of those at home holds no true weight, now or ever, what matters is that those that surround you at this moment will share your triumph and horror alike; care for what they think and know that if you respect your oath to them... to me, you will have acted honorably. That is the most any of us can hope for, for in the end, it is the only thing with meaning. They will make you heroes, but you will make yourself worthy." The shadows in my mind taunted me, denying everything I said. I ruthlessly subdued them.

II.

The following weeks were spent in zealous training, my soldiers excelling at every task. Yet I pushed them ever harder, honing their skills beyond mere proficiency to near perfection. I had no choice. The emperor's scouts had brought back word of the enemy's movement. Soon we would all see battle.

But this was not what chilled my blood and sent shivers down my spine. Night by night a misty escort accompanied me into sleep, betrayed by a shadow, the muted echo of languidly beating wings, a sudden cackle, a shrill scream.

New nightmares came to me each time I sought to rest. Born on the biting winds off of the sea, they wreathed my slumber in terror and torment and ecstasy. Images of battle... of death... my men spread like dead flies upon the ground. Over and over I watched them, both haunted-eyed soldiers and fresh young faces not yet scarred by battle; all turned their gaze toward foreign shores. Their trust in me was complete. Their trust in me was damning. In the darkness of my own mind, I watched my men die, savaged by a faceless enemy, their entrails strewn across countless battlefields, their lifeless eyes trailing me accusingly as I picked my way past their corpses and waded through mud made black with their shed blood.

My dream-self closed its eyes, but the images could not be shut out. Neither could the screams. It was the torment of their souls consumed by terror, agony unleashed in endless shivering waves.

Each morning I woke atremble, my eyes hollow pits, my skin pale beneath its soldier's weathering. More times than I could count, I woke at my own cry, "I have failed them, they are all dead!"

Only my aide knew of this, and his dedication kept him silent.

I struggled to thrust my unease from me. My troops may have been the Emperor's chosen, but their own excellence has kept them here. I have not trained them to die. The dreams were nothing but my doubts manifest... my own unreasonable doubts.

Among the ranks, I marched like a demon possessed, my countenance fierce, my temperament demanding, while inside my breast my heart died a little more every day. My forces were pushed to excel at every skill demanded of them. I watched on, a not-so-silent goad, and even my captains did not know which to fear more: our uncertain future, or me.

"You're overextending, Thalon... Get your stance back in line, find your center and do not stray from it; our foe will not be as forgiving as Ghin here is." My words were stern but encouraging as I addressed my aide. I lingered a moment, to watch his next attempt, or so I intended until I spied another among the ranks, his gear an affront to my warrior's sensibilities.

Brief flashes of my nightmares swiftly rose up at the sight, until I barked and snapped most ferociously at the man, "Your armor is an outrage, soldier, whoever taught you such inept care must wish you dead, or you've a wish all your own to gain the other side. I want each plate repaired, in order, and properly assembled before you seek your pallet tonight!"

I ignored the confused and angry flush of half the sergeants surrounding me. They wondered what rode me. I wondered as well, but I forced myself not to care. I would not have even one recruit fall because we failed to train them sufficiently. If their pride was scarred, let them renew their efforts to prepare as best they could.

My blood pulsed like a caged beast seeking escape as I continued to tour the ranks. My eyes took on a wild cast and my breathing grew harsh. Everywhere faces from my dreams confronted me. Passing each man, a fleeting image of their dream-deaths cloaked their features in gruesome effigy. Throats slashed to the bone, eyes dangling wetly from their sockets, blood welling from mouths even now calling out the training chants that continued to fill my ears with unfailing precision. The vicious mocking did not end.

I felt cornered. Every step I took, haunting whispers followed me, venomous and faint; ghostly screams floating on the breeze, apparently for me alone. My teeth clenched, stifling an answering groan and it was all I could do to keep myself from whirling around in an attempt to spy my tormentor.

Was this madness? Growling, my heart sought the darkness within. I would wrestle it down and raze it from my being. Shooting a look at my second in command, I left the field to him, stalking off toward the shore to war with my demons.

III.

The blue-grey sand sparkled like crushed gems in the dying light of the day. I had not realized the lateness of the hour. How much better I understood my restlessness. I had lost all desire for sleep, though not the need.

I had managed to work up a thick sheen of sweat in pacing my men. Taking myself to the water's edge, I reached down to scoop up a bit of an incoming wave. Raising it, I stayed my hand mere moments from dousing my head; a shadow crept across the sun, stealing its brilliance, muting its setting glory, and a whispering flutter of leathery wings danced around the edge of my hearing. I trembled without shame.

The seawater was sluggish in my palm and lacked the sharp crispness I had always found so refreshing. A stench unimaginable wafted from the puddle in my hand and from the surf at my feet. I was no green recruit... I was a seasoned warrior and I have smelt death. Yet looking down, instead of the blood and offal I expected, I spied a thick green slime coating my hand. Foreboding shot through me.

There was a gleeful cackling in my thoughts as I dashed the sludge away, biting off a curse. Looking wild-eyed at the surf, I nearly cackled myself... madly. The surf was as crisp and clean as the day the gods had wept it. There was nothing in the sand where I had cast my handful. This was madness! With my eyes closed and my jaw and every other muscle clenched, I began my private war.

"They are but dreams!" I roared. "They have no power over me that I do not allow them! You are nothing but unfounded doubt! You are senseless fear! You are nothing but fancy!"

Sweeping out my practice blade, I whirled on the battered, but stout log buried there in the sand. Towering over my head, it was my own private practice post and I attacked it with a vengeance. Over and over my blade fell with ruthless force.

"Nothing! No screams! No death! No goddamn fluttering wings! Nothing, do you hear me?"

I descended into obsession, no longer rational enough for words; I punctuated each punishing slash with a formless cry. Rage poured through me and out along my blade.

"Ggrr... ggggrrrr. Augh!"

My muscles burned and my skin stretched taut; I dreaded the rumbling *swish* of the surf, for the little I could distinguish beneath my roars hinted at nasty, triumphant whispers.

"AuuuGGH!! Augh... Augh... AauuuggH!"

My heart thudded mercilessly against my breastbone and my breath tripped over itself in its haste. Grayness swarmed my vision and I continued to growl through clenched teeth as I turned to confront the sea. With all my escalating fury I stumbled forward and cast my wooden practice blade like a spear into its depths. As if such a pathetic weapon could pierce the heart of the darkness I sensed writhing there. I would regret that wastefulness later. For now, I watched intently as it lanced through the sky and impaled the ocean smoothly, forcefully. Yet nothing rose up from the depths but a brief splash, and my blade was gone. I fell to my knees and felt like weeping as the waves chuckled at my powerless obsession.

I was too spent to care, too worn by weeks of restless nights, left drained by my futile exertions. I fell forward in the sand, letting the waves wash over me, wanting to scream at their deceptive sweetness. Something was foul here, I thought as unconsciousness claimed me. It was merely well hidden.

IV.

Torn limbs drifted by me on knee-high waves of blood. A body lurked beneath the surface, reaching out to me, as I passed, with half a green-glowing hand; there was no head, just splinters of gnawed bone and white cartilage rising from the tattered remains of one of my sergeant's necks.

I should have known him. Even without a face, I should have known him. As things were, it was only his torque—amazingly still in place—that confessed his rank.

As I walked the battlefield, my useless sword dangling from fingers long numb, I could feel the shadow following me. No...

they were legion, not just one. Something brushed my back, taunting, and the *shushing* of flexing wings filled the silence left by the carnage. What were they waiting for? My forces lay obliterated around me, their screams still echoed endlessly in my mind. Why did they not come for me?

"They are all dead! I have failed them!" Chuckling glee was my only answer, *he-he, he-he, he-he...* building like a pulse. It was maddening until I could bear the torment no more...

V.

The voices in my head were now deep and rumbling. They did not trouble themselves to hide on the fringes of my thoughts... they didn't bother to tease and taunt... The voices called me forth from my sleep.

Ph-nglui mglw'nafh Cthulu R'lyeh
wgah'nagl fhtagn... Cthulu fhtagn

Gibberish, complete gibberish. But that did not stop my blood from turning to ice. I fought the compulsion to repeat the phrase. To let the words fall off my tongue as they desired to. What did it mean? Relentless... ominous... I could not evade the dread those words evoked in me, regardless of my inability to comprehend them.

Opening my eyes, some oddity of the moonlight cast a green glow upon the water. It quickly faded, as I blinked away sleep. All save in one spot. Rearing up onto my knees, I stared at the glowing depression in the sand. The moon was nowhere near full and did not offer enough light for me to distinguish what rested there.

What I should not have been able to see called to me in sibilant whispers, speaking to my soul. The promises were both horrific and tempting, again offering me the terror and torment and ecstasy of my dreams. The darkness in my heart trembled eagerly. The rest of me cringed away.

Crouching in the sands, my sensibilities rebelled. My hand shook as I did battle with it. The dream visions of the weeks past rose again unbidden as I lost my struggle and tentatively reached out, not quite brushing the heavy, gold-swirled statue cradled in the sand before me. The cold intensified before my skin even touched the stygian darkness of the unknown mineral. Revulsion gripped me and my stomach rebelled like a raw recruit's. My soul took one step back from damnation.

Staring up at me, coldly calculating, was a hand-high statuette washed ashore by the treacherous waves. A pair of dark, depthless eyes perched above tentacles that gave the illusion of being poised to lash out at me. A half-remembered dream image told me they would be thicker than my well-muscled thigh, my waist even, were this creature to stand before me... or, I should say, over me. The head, in proportion, was enormous and shaped as a familiar creature from the sea, only attached to a powerful body that would dwarf my own several times over, once again, were we face to face.

The reflection of this thing haunted my sleep, the broken bodies of my men scattered like grains of rice at its feet. Its size alone would have made me quail, though it galled me to admit it even to myself... but the sight of the lethal claws biting into the rune-covered pedestal it perched upon left me shaken as my mind easily calculated their likely length. I could well imagine what a natural complement of weapons such as these could do to my men.

Yet even with all of this, it was the massive wings folded cloak-like down the creature's back that told me I had spied my demon at last.

The wind sniggered yet again, and my fury returned full-force, banishing my doubt. With a swift swoop, I cupped my hand under the wet sand where the idol sat—nothing could bring me to touch the hateful thing directly—and rising, drew back my arm and flung the handful back into the sea.

Only as it disappeared from sight did I notice what could only be the fierce dragon prows favored by the Empire's mortal enemy, just now rising over the horizon. The eve of battle was upon us. I knew both thrill and fear.

I could feel the wing-whipped wind howl at my back as I stalked away. My very soul quaked as it encompassed me. I watched in horror as it reflected my image back at me, until I no longer recognized the man staring back.

VI.

"Rise up!" I bellowed loudly as I entered the camp, my expression grim as I took the sentries by surprise. Quick anger heated my words and my eyes flashed cold, glimmering briefly with a green glow in the dark, if only for a moment. They would pay later for their inattention. For now, dawn was mere hours away, and I intended we would be on the march long before the sun lit the sky. "Fall out and formation in fifteen!"

Officers aligned themselves beside their squads and battalions with precision. Without a word, I stood before them as my aide dressed me in my armor. I forced my eyes not to follow the hulking shadows that darted among the ranks. Ever since my slumber on the beach I had their images to add to my torment. They taunted me as I addressed my men.

"The enemy approaches; within two hours they will be upon our shore. We will not meet them on a battlefield of their choosing. Gather your gear, we march within the quarter hour and lead them to where we make our stand. The advantage is ours, men, let us press it."

The shadows mocked me, replacing my forces once again with the death-images from my dreams. They played on the doubts I'd struggled to eradicate. Rage filled me, pushing out my fears. They were senseless! They did not exist! Yet their sniggers grew deeper into all-out, mocking laughter as Thalon handed me my battle blade.

VII.

As we made our way through misty vales, I listened to the *thump-thump-thump-thump* all around me... the horses' hooves... the marching of my men... my quickening pulse. It was as if we made our way across the inside of a drum, rather than into the fiery red glow of approaching dawn.

We were close. I halted at a rise and waited for my forces to draw up to me. I had always known where I would bring them for this battle that they might draw upon the might of those who came before. Ahead of me, laid out in that instant for my eyes alone, was the Forest of a Thousand Lost Souls.

No trees materialized from the morning fog. This was a copse of corpses, or what was left of them. A thousand colossal souls found their final rest in this place. For miles, their twisted and broken limbs of aged bone rose up like giants, as high as three men each standing atop the other. Those massive skulls still in place were thrown back upon their neck bones in endless, eternal screams. Side by side with the bones, the armaments of fallen warriors pierced the sky, dwarfing our forces as we stood in their shadow; maces and lances, swords and two-handed axes... every weapon ever imagined planted in the ground reaching heavenward... each one of a size to suit a Titan.

I could feel the souls, daring me, measuring my worth on first impression. My face remained impassive as I stood at the head of my army with justifiable pride. We were worthy to walk among those fallen, to add our legend to theirs... to surpass it, in fact, as I would not... could not believe my army would fail.

In the back of my mind the shadows deepened and surged, and my battle lust demanded blood, though I reined it in with the same command I wielded with my men. I turned as my officers drew their mounts beside mine. Awe mingled with the reverence in their gazes. Glancing behind me, my eyes trailed across their ranks.

My men did not disappoint. Satisfied, I began my descent into the valley. Wending our way through the vast forest of bleached bone and weapons that edged the plain was no easy chore, but as I drew closer to my goal I was overcome by the magnitude of our undertaking. Surely, surrounded by the souls of these valiant dead, we would find our might amplified tenfold... nay, a hundred fold.

For once the whispers were drowned out. My demons could not overcome the clamoring voices of the dead from a thousand wars. Their screams were rich and strangely savory. The echoes of their ancient battle cries thrummed through my veins. They kept pace with my rapid pulse... almost time.

I could sense the foe drawing near, poised and ready to strike, but unfathomably holding back. It was as if I could hear the pounding of their march in my very bones. I could feel a hint of battlelust steal over me like an ever-increasing itch.

VIII.

I barely took note of the furtive looks the soldiers cast in my direction at the continued absence of our foe. I was lost in the ever-shifting parade of ancient dead. I found myself the center of sifting spirals as the shadows and the legends bound and counter-bound me in their swirling energies.

Before my inner eye flashed the glory of past battles. I wanted this for my men, to blood them in triumph, to set them forever above all other fighting men. I would become immortal!

From deep inside me, my soul screamed in outrage at my thoughts, so opposite my own philosophy. The rest of me was deaf to those cries. Instead, my languid gaze followed as the carrion crows flew by. I relished the sound of flapping wings. They could feel the tension; they could read the signs. They cawed their impatience at our unmoving stance, eager to feast upon the anticipated spoils. My aide flinched as a bird's cry sounded from above him. At the sight, sudden, inexplicable rage boiled through me, and the conflicting battle between my nature and my actions was finally lost.

Flinched! How dare the man count himself a member of my ranks with so faint a store of courage? He was my chosen, most favored of the common soldiers, personally groomed by myself to one day take his place among my officers. It was a disgrace!

Swiftly I charged, kneeing my stallion to the site of my army's blemish. Weakness could not be tolerated; weakness would drag the whole body down. Retribution was as swift as my mount, and as sharp as my blade.

Crimson stained my view once more as my sword came away bathed in Thalon's blood and I shivered at the cool caress of death. The silence took on the weight of a collective gasp, a quickly quelled cry of outrage.

My blue eyes glimmered green. Tremors rippled through me as surging death cloaked me in ineffable power. The coil drew tighter. The shadows deepened, the thumping pulse quickened, and anticipation was heavy in the air. The whispers rose into a shouted triumph and an eldritch glow crept over the battlefield, encompassing the deadly forest.

No one moved, nor was it likely they were able to. I found myself looking out upon the sky as an unholy light gathered above my head. It pulsed with power, a power that repulsed me even as I lusted after it. I had to feel its embrace. The splendor it promised... I would be a hero.

No! That wasn't right... I was not here to be a hero; but still, I reached up my hand. I was doomed. As the radiance sheathed my hand it set the rest of me glowing in a haze of glory. Nothing was left of the man I'd been.

I looked out and I could see them, the shadows surrounded my army, tangible nightmares rising up in their horrendous magnificence. I grew taut with anticipation. I waited for the dream-images to be fulfilled.

Dark, depthless eyes burned with hunger and tentacles lashed in frenzy. Rank upon rank upon rank of powerful beings stood before me, dwarfing the mortal men. They each resembled my little, cast-away idol.

I heard the screams, indistinguishable from those of my dreams. It relieved me to once again be fully immersed in the jarring auditory assault. I had grown so used to it.

I looked back down at my hand... it burned. I discovered my flesh scorched black as a void. The darkness crept up my limb and oblivion drew closer. From its depths, my nightmare laughed back at me.

My gaze drifted to my soldiers. Looming shadows tore them limb from body and flesh from bone. Numbly, I noticed I had underestimated the length of those talons. One pierced the last of my sergeants through his head, the wicked curve protruding from the man's belly.

It was true then: Every one of them is dead...

IX.

The copper-penny stench of blood hung in the air as it dripped from my blade.

I stood in stillness broken only occasionally by squabbling ravens, watching as the shadow-creatures sank once again into the cursed soil. As I looked at my men, I struggled to find the dividing line between my nightmares and reality. The ranks were assembled, patiently awaiting the arrival of the enemy...

the enemy who only now surged along the perimeter of the battleground.

No one moved.

Shocked murmurs shattered the silence and a single voice rose from the approaching horde, "My god! What happened here?"

A solitary scout crept onto the plain, stopping at the edges of my assembly, circling, but going no deeper. His face grew paler than the moon as I watched him wheel abruptly and lope away, straight back to his commander.

"They are all dead, sir, slaughtered in their ranks." His voice trembled and I wondered that I could hear him at all, but it didn't matter. My satisfaction grew as I heard mutters of "cursed land" and "ill omens." I knew the thrill of triumph as the enemy forces turned about and marched away with haste. The field was ours; the enemy would not stand against us.

I took my place in the Forest of a Thousand and One Lost Souls, my head thrown back in a cry of ecstasy, my bare bones gleaming in the weak light that occasionally broke through the clouds. I am larger than life... a legend, my mighty sword a monolith beside me, my head thrown back in a cry of terror.

Uncast Shadows

WE ARE THE UNCAST SHADOWS. THE THOUGHTS YOU DARE NOT acknowledge, the dreams you dare not pursue, the fears and regrets of a thousand lifetimes. We are what you are unable to admit and you cannot elude. You feel us in your very marrow, cutting at your skin as if we would seep out the wounds and leave you free. Do you feel alive? It's a lie.

You lose a little more of yourself each time you do.

"Go away. You aren't real, you don't exist!"

You'd like to think so, wouldn't you? It doesn't work that way. Look at us. Go on... look... Do you find us familiar? Disturbingly so, I'm sure. It is your face upon every one of us. The one you hide beneath; the endless masks you show the world.

You will not look away! We have been disregarded long enough. We surround you, hem you in on every side until you can scarcely draw breath. That's right. Whimper. Pant. Piss yourself as you catch even a glimpse of what is inside of you. Of what we are. What do we care? Our noses are deadened to all but the ever-present stench of rot. Soured dreams, putrid thoughts, moral decay.

"This isn't happening. No... this isn't happening."

Isn't it? Place your hand on your chest. Feel your rapid-fire pulse. Feel the clammy clinging of the gown. The trembling of your flesh... Look at us! You will see. You will concede. We exist. We will not be ignored. Do you think that pounding on your skull will drown us out? We could whisper on but a breath and still it would echo in your head. We could scream at the top of your lungs and not another would hear. There is not a space inside you we do not fill. Nowhere to hide, nowhere to escape. Not within this skin.

Or perhaps that is the problem? It binds you too tight, locks you in the here-and-now, anchors you. Don't you think?

Shed it. Strip it away. Pick at it like a scab until it loosens. Peel until you are free of it. It's only patchwork anyway, beneath the surface, where none can see... The pieces come away so easily. Come... let us help you...

An Alliance Archives Adventure

On the command deck of the Stellar Clipper *McKay*, First Officer Ushimi Yakata ran the final checklist before third shift ended:

DUTY LOG: 42.05.18 – 0715HRS, YAKATA, U.

> Reactor status – nominal;
> O2 levels – optimal;
> Power – five percent over-consumption.

She frowned at the last item as she printed out a hard copy of the entry. *We're going to have to watch our calculations,* she thought. *We haven't even left orbit and already the systems are running hot.*

It was that damn shuttle Corporate had them balancing on the *McKay*'s nose. They were hauling the spacer's equivalent of a luxury yacht over twelve light years to Demeter just so some CEO could tour his colonial facilities in style... There were much more important payloads they could have taken with them. Of course, it was the "pay" part that decided things in the end; the rates for transporting luxury items to the Tau Ceti system were ten times that of necessary goods.

Behind her a *clunk* and a soft *whoosh* announced the arrival of her replacement. A whiff of licorice drifted from close by her ear. She'd stopped counting the times she had told Karl Dunn not to crowd her. A prime example of why they had a history and no future. She'd had doubts about signing him for this cruise. They had been close once, very close. But not anymore. And with only a nine-man crew, she had no hope of avoiding him.

Her lips pressed in a tight, thin line, Yakata dropped her hand to the toggle by her hip and shifted the command chair back along its track, away from the control panel.

"Hey! Watch it!"

She brought the chair around, her grey eyes leveled dead on at Karl as he rubbed his abdomen where the chair smacked into him. Only his grip on the nearby tether bar kept him bobbing in place.

"Excuse me," she said, her tone cool and formal. "I didn't realize you were so close."

The flat, persistent tone of the proximity warning sounded through the cabin, interrupting any comment Karl would have made. They both forgot their personal conflict, their attention riveted on the sensors.

Toggling the command chair back into place, Yakata automatically scanned the ship's attitude and power consumption on the screens flanking the main monitor. At the same time, she called up the isometric collision display. The flashing alert icon vanished from the screen in front of her. In its place appeared a wire-frame sphere with a representation of the McKay in the center. Something closed on the ship from behind, moving at a fraction of a meter per second. They had about thirty minutes until it came into range over their drive section.

"Dunn, reach over and activate the aft camera," Yakata ordered as her fingers danced in and out of the button depressions on the control panel. At her command, the main display switched from short-range to long-range scanning. She had to be sure whatever approached was not the forward edge of a meteor storm or something else their ablative hull plating could not handle.

Her scans told her nothing more.

She called to Karl, "Crewman, do we have visual?"

Silence.

"Crewman..." Her short, sharp tone telegraphed impatience. "Do... we... have... visual?"

She whipped around, spearing him with a glare. He remained oblivious, his feet tucked into the boot docks and his gaze riveted on the image on the external monitoring station.

What the hell? Yakata had never seen him like this. He looked stunned... horrified. What could be out there?

Remembering the fate of her father's freighter, the *Tyler*, she felt a shiver of dread. Not another wreck...

She couldn't tell; Karl's body blocked the screen. Impatiently, she released the restraint keeping her in the command chair and drifted out. Once she cleared the panel, she rotated and pulled herself toward Karl.

"Step aside, crewman," she barked.

His intent gaze snapped to her. Emotions rippled violently across his face, darkening his deep brown eyes to nearly black. It unsettled her, but Yakata didn't back off. Dunn's moods were nothing new to her. He had always been too on edge, his emotions close to the surface; like he picked up on random vibes in the air that no one else could feel. In their time together, she had never been able to tell what a given situation would trigger. Now she told herself she didn't really care. She kept her expression impassive and her gaze sharp. "Move it... now."

The muscles along Karl's jaw twitched and his eyes fell out of focus. He closed them and gave his head a little shake. She could see the tension drain away. When he opened his eyes again, they reflected faint confusion. Without a word, he gave the standard heel jerk to free his feet from the workstation's dock and drifted off to the side.

She gave him a measured look before redirecting her attention to the screen. The camera completed deployment, the high-power, one-hundred-optical zoom fully engaged. What a stunning view. Distant stars glittered like metallic flecks on a field of raw black silk and muted colors added an unexpected depth to the starscape. Pretty sights didn't interest her, though. She scanned for her objective with an intensity that mirrored Karl's earlier stance.

The projectile headed toward them wasn't some random bit of space debris; it was clearly manufactured. The shape appeared something like a squat pillar or obelisk, and appeared to be about the size of her head. It was too far away to make out much more, though the camera hinted at intricate detail.

Rogue thoughts of her father swarmed her mind once more. In his last letter to her, he mentioned a similar find. She'd lost him long before the letter ever reached her. Neither her father, nor the object had been retrieved. Burned into her memory, as clear as yesterday, was the image of his shattered helmet found floating in the vacuum of space. She still had that helmet.

She banished the thought. Turning back to Karl, Yakata caught his eye and held it. "Assume your post. I'm heading up to the rendezvous station to retrieve the object."

He remained silent a moment. His jaw ticked and his gaze flickered from the aft display to her face.

"'Ta...'" he began, but she cut him off.

"Excuse me, crewman, how did you address me?"

"Ma'am," he ground out through clenched teeth, frustration snapping in his eyes. "Respectfully, I'm not sure that you should... something feels really wrong about this."

"I have to do this."

The knowing look he gave her disconcerted Yakata. If anyone understood, he did. She didn't like that familiarity or the self-betraying warmth she felt at his concern. "I said get to your post. Start the pre-hyperdrive checklist," she ordered. "The captain wants to jump by 0800."

She pulled her communications hood up over her close-cropped ebony hair and triggered the overhead hatch. With the grace of frequent practice, she hauled herself up through the shaft. Propelling herself past the T-junction that branched off toward the cargo bay, she opened the second hatch into the rendezvous station. She closed it behind her before drifting toward the aft window. Yakata pressed the activation button on the left side of her comm hood. "Command deck..."

A sharp chirp sounded before Karl responded, his voice slightly staticky. "Go ahead, ma'am."

"I need an update on the incoming object."

There was a pause. While she waited, Yakata peered out into space, as if she had any chance of pinpointing the object without the aid of the cameras. It drew closer, but not that close.

Another chirp brought her out of her distraction.

"Ma'am?"

"Go ahead, crewman."

"The object is ten minutes out and closing."

"Acknowledged," she responded, and cut the connection.

Ten minutes. Barely enough time to deploy the arm. She snapped her boots into the docks and engaged the control panel. Powering up the arm, she then hit the sequence instructing it to retrieve the grappling attachment. While the mechanism prepared, she triggered the cargo bay doors. A strident warning klaxon sounded as a large segment of the ship opened to space. The arm rose from its cradle in slow, precise movements. Her teeth gritted and her muscles tensed as she watched. It had to move faster or she would miss the interception point. With her free hand, she depressed the activator on her comm hood once more.

"Command deck..."

"Go ahead, ma'am."

"Feed me the trajectory of the object."

On the panel in front of her, a micro-display came to life. The information played across it. This was going to be close. She deployed the grappling net to intersect the flight path and held her breath. The object crested the drive section in a gentle arc, and seemed to flare as it came into contact with the sun's rays, bathing the ship and arm in a startling green glow. It faded in the shadow of the arm. Yakata leaned into the console. It appeared her prize might overshoot the net. Reaching for the joystick in front of her, she extended the assembly as high as it would go over the drive section.

Her breath hitched. It still looked at risk of skimming past. *This is ridiculous. It's space debris. There's no reason I should be so upset.* She tried shifting the joystick even further, but the arm had reached full extension.

Her father's face drifted unbidden across her thoughts. It felt like she had failed him... again. She clenched her teeth and forced the thought away. Furious blinking cleared her vision, but she could hardly believe what she saw: the object changed trajectory. The alteration was slight; barely perceptible except for the drive section acting as a point of reference. Still, Yakata had to wonder if she had really seen it. This was impossible. The thing could not have changed its trajectory. Short of mechanical means or an outside intervention, an object moving in space would continue along the same path until it encountered another force. And yet, as the artifact plowed into the grappling net, she forgot all about the laws of physics. The net closed, locking the object into place.

"Yeah!" she cried out, the sound loud and unbridled in the seclusion of the rendezvous station. Only the boot docks kept her from bouncing around the compartment. "Oh, yeah!"

A burst of unexpected static crackled from her comm hood. She felt the blood drain from her face as she went still.

"Hey! Knock it off!" Karl's amused voice came over the connection she'd forgotten to close. "You want to rupture my ear drum?"

"My apologies, crewman," she responded with a degree of dignity she did not currently feel. "The object has been retrieved. I'm locking down and securing the salvage."

She cut the connection.

Shoving embarrassment aside, Yakata input the sequence that returned the arm to its cradle. Another rapid set of keystrokes, and the cargo bay doors closed. She grew impatient with the drawn-out procedure. Recklessness in vacuum, however, could get a spacer killed.

Once everything was locked down, she retreated to the antechamber to climb into her protective constrictor suit. She waited for the green light from the automatic systems check before securing her helmet and engaging the O_2 tanks. Prepped for EVA, Yakata cycled through the airlock into the cargo bay.

She grabbed an empty storage container and hauled both it and herself down the length of the armature. Once there, she anchored the container to the deck and pulled herself up the handholds along the wall until she drew even with the grappling attachment. She hit the release and worked the fingers open.

Her hands twitched over the surface of the artifact and she had to resist the urge to draw off her suit's skin-tight gloves. The object demanded to be caressed.

In shape, it resembled a short, squat obelisk. It tapered slightly from top to bottom and had three columns of unfamiliar symbols running up and down each side. It was metal... apparently old metal, given the deep, dull sheen. The color had a greenish tinge, like ancient bronze. Only this was no metal she recognized. It seemed smooth, almost soft, other than the etching. Otherwise, there were no seams or depressions.

It took extreme effort to lower the thing into the bin. Now was not the time to examine it. She had less than ten minutes to get herself secured for hyperdrive. Unhitching the container, she hefted it to her shoulder and propelled herself toward the airlock. In the antechamber, she slid her burden into a storage locker by the cargo bay hatch and keyed it to her personal code. It would be safe until she could take it down to the lab.

DUTY LOG: 42.05.18 – 1100HRS, KINNEY, CAPTAIN J.

Reactor status – nominal;
O2 levels – 98 percent;
Power – ten percent over-consumption

Note: Schedule diagnostics of ship's systems upon arrival at Demeter, McKay exhibiting systems-wide reduction in efficiency despite recent overhaul. Power fluctuations ship-wide, stabilized. Malfunction of atmospheric filters in compartments 8A through C, corrected. Electrical fires between bulkheads 10 and 11, section 5, contained; damage minimal.

CARGO BAY ANTECHAMBER: 42.05.18 – 1100HRS

Yakata struggled for hours to get some rest, but found no success. The artifact haunted her thoughts. She would almost say it called to her, but that was as nuts as thinking it had changed its trajectory. She tossed and fussed until Jackson and Pittman, the crewmembers trying to sleep in the billets flanking hers, begged her to give up.

That was why she climbed back down into the cargo bay antechamber again. Captain Kinney, in position on the command deck, had given her a considering look, but didn't question her. She'd already briefed him about the events that occurred at the end of her shift.

All thought of anything but the artifact fled her mind as she pushed open the last hatch and continued down the ladder, which in orbit had been the floor. She hated the way hyperdrive and the artificial gravity it created turned reality perpendicular to orbital conditions. Kneeling down, she punched her code with rapid jabs and hauled open the storage locker at her feet.

Any thought of spatial geometry evaporated.

Yakata half expected the artifact to be a dream. But there it was, nestled in its bin. She tried to draw it out of the locker.

It wouldn't budge. In the weightlessness of the orbiting ship, the artifact had been nothing to move. Now that they were under drive there was artificial gravity again. Not earth-norm, but enough that they could walk on the deck. If the obelisk was this heavy in three-quarters grav, she didn't want to consider what it would be like under normal conditions. It had to be denser than gold.

No! Yakata straddled the opening, flexed her knees, and inch by inch pulled the container up, until sweat ran into her eyes and her muscles screamed. She was not waiting forty-eight hours until they were in orbit.

PERSONAL LOG ENTRY: 42.05.18 – 1230HRS, DUNN, K.

We retrieved something today. 'Ta... excuse me... First Officer Ushimi hasn't told me what it is. Don't think she even knows. While I was on shift, she took it to the storage bay Captain had temporarily converted into a lab. She talked O'Neal, the metallurgist we're shepherding to Demeter, into helping her try to figure out what it is.

She goes on shift in seven hours, but they're still holed up in that lab. She's going to be a real bitch on deck tonight if she doesn't get some sleep, but she's obsessing on that bit of debris.

Of course, I can't stop thinking about it either. It's gotten under my skin. It shouldn't be on this ship! It has me so freaked, and I can't even tell why. The first half-hour of my shift is a lost memory. All I know is that it feels like we are in for a major shitstorm.

Temporary Science Lab: 42.05.18 – 1230hrs

"What in the world made Corporate think it was worth the 100-million-dollar ticket to haul you up here?" Yakata growled through clenched teeth. Even as she said it, her hindbrain winced.

Bastian O'Neal, world-renowned metallurgist, lowered his instruments to the work surface and gave her a long, silent look. The dignified expression on his ebony face didn't change, but his hazel eyes were disapproving. He didn't answer. He looked away and took up the artifact in both latex-covered hands, repositioning it for another documenting photograph.

She'd strained to haul her prize down here; he seemed to toss it about as if it were cotton candy. Part of that was due to his clearly prosthetic left arm; but part had to be because of his own innate strength. Someone who didn't know better could be excused for thinking he mined metals, rather than studying them.

The metallurgist set aside his digital camera and picked up the item once more. He turned it in his hands until he'd looked at every side, his finger lingered over the engraving. She wanted to snatch it from his grasp. Uncontrollably, a muscle in her forehead twitched, as did her fingers. How dare he manhandle her salvage like that, hefting it with an ease that she couldn't? She tensed and fought not to scowl at him. What was wrong with her?

Yakata tried to shake it off. This was O'Neal's field. She'd come to him for help and he was kind enough to give it. She should be grateful and respectful, at the very least. It wasn't like her to behave this way. She took a deep breath and forced herself to calm, to offer an apologetic smile and be pleasant.

Finally, O'Neal set the artifact down. Yakata expected to relax. Instead, she tensed even more; ready, in fact, to hurry forward and grab the obelisk away. But then O'Neal spoke, distracting her.

"I can't identify it."

"What do you mean you can't identify it?!"

"The tests were unable to determine the age or composition of the material."

Her resolve to be polite evaporated. "What did Corporate do... send you up here as a tax write-off?"

Seething with frustration, Yakata grabbed for her artifact.

O'Neal stepped in her way.

"If you're done insulting me?

"There's one more test I can run, but I need some equipment from the storage bay. My imaging spectrometer is our last option on-ship."

She glared at him and had to force her negativity down. It was harder to do. Without a word, Yakata moved to the terminal set into the chamber wall, her feet straddling the boot docks.

The muscles in her shoulders bunched and tightened as she keyed in the commands calling up the ship's manifest. He watched her. Surely plotting to take her salvage for himself.

Whoa! Where did that paranoia come from? She forced it away.

Finally, she located his equipment and requested immediate retrieval. Closing out the screen, she whirled to face him. For a moment, everything held a greenish tinge like the one she'd noted when the object crested the drive section. The sense of looming increased with the glow. It faded so quickly, though, that she had to wonder if it were her vision causing the effect. That would explain the flickers out of the corner of her eye. Yakata clenched her eyes shut and popped her neck. It sounded like several rounds of gunfire.

"Sorry, O'Neal, can't imagine why I'm so edgy. Jackson will bring your spectrometer down in short order. Why don't you head to the mess for some coffee... I'll comm you when the equipment gets here."

"That's okay. If I'm here when it arrives, I can hook it into the ship's systems quicker. This has already taken longer..."

"O'Neal," Yakata cut him off, her tone sharp and brittle, even to her own ears. "Go get some coffee. I'll have the spectrometer rigged up when you get here."

For a moment, she thought he would refuse. Her suspicions flared brighter and she had to consciously force her fists not to clench. She didn't trust him here; didn't want him here, unless he was in the middle of a test. Even then she had issues.

Her gaze again locked with his. She read concern in his eyes. But did something else lurk beneath that? Something sly? Calculating? Damnit! She couldn't tell! It took more effort to mimic something of a reasonable tone. "I have to be here to sign off on the retrieval. If you don't want any coffee, could you at least get me some? I'm dying here."

TEMPORARY SCIENCE LAB: 42.05.18 – 1245HRS

Yakata vibrated with impatience as O'Neal finished calibrating the spectrometer. She wanted to snatch his hands away from the knobs and buttons and yell at him to get on with it. It wasn't just an overwhelming need to know. That she could have handled. No, it was more like whatever lurked behind her drew closer, just out of sight, just out of hearing range. Always there, always watching... Some part of her equated it with the artifact. She had to know what it was now, but the technology would do them no good if it weren't set up properly. She understood that.

Then why was she ready to scream when he slipped a common bit of steel in the spherical sample chamber and fired up the machine?

She couldn't restrain herself anymore. "Come on, already!"

"Do you want accurate results, or do you just want me to go through the motions?" O'Neal's voice came out a low, controlled rumble, contrasting sharply with her outburst. "If you don't care if the results are accurate, you're wasting my time and I'm out of here."

His response made Yakata want to scream even more, but he was right. What was wrong with her? Her impatience did not serve either one of them well and she couldn't afford to have him abandon the test. She could probably figure out the machine, but the data it spit out would be indecipherable to her.

Taking a deep breath, she forced herself to calm.

"Sorry."

It took a lot of effort not to fidget as O'Neal watched her closely a moment. The concern had returned, along with a thread of irritation. He clearly wanted this to be done as much as she did, even if their reasons were different. Without a word, he turned back to the spectrometer.

"Okay, we're ready."

Yakata's pulse sped up. She reached for the artifact, only to flinch back as a mild static arced between it and her fingertips.

It seemed to cling to her hand like the persistent suction of vacuum through a hull breach. Like something tried to suck her out the tiniest hole, only the hard surface of reality kept her from going through. Before she could say something, the pull abruptly released and a surge of rage and frustration swelled over her. She shook it off. Looked up in a daze. O'Neal had lifted her prize away and slid it into the chamber in place of the metal bar. He made no comment and Yakata saw no sparks when he touched it. Had the phenomenon been her imagination? She couldn't resist creeping forward to glance at the operator's display as the spectrometer charged up to pulse full-spectrum light at the object from six points within the sphere.

The hum of the machine seemed to come up through the deck plates until she expected her entire body to vibrate with it. A flaring light intensified abruptly until it engulfed the machine and the room. The power surged and the deck plates vibrated more violently beneath Yakata's feet. Both she and O'Neal flinched in that instance of brilliance before they were engulfed by utter darkness. A sharp gasp broke the silence. She couldn't tell which of them it came from. She could no longer hear the spectrometer or any of the ship's normal background mechanical noises. Other than their nervous breathing, silence dominated the pitch black.

Yakata struggled not to panic. Where was the hum of the hyperdrive? The click of relays opening and closing? The sizzling snap of the comms? Sounds every spacer took for granted; their unrealized security blanket in everlasting night.

Yakata shuddered.

The darkness seemed to last forever; in truth it was less than twenty seconds before systems re-engaged with a whir. Not even long enough for them to fall out of drive.

Right on the heels of everything powering up, all comms within hearing distance gave a strident chirp.

"...eport... All crew, report!"

She reached for the comm on the console and toggled the activator to respond to Captain Kinney.

"Yakata here. O'Neal and I are in the Science Lab."

"What the hell was that?"

Yakata didn't have an answer. She couldn't have gotten one in, anyway, as a stream of responses came over the comm. All crew were accounted for.

"Everyone to stations, run full diagnostics. Let's figure out what the deal is before it happens again," Captain Kinney ordered before closing the comm line.

Turning to O'Neal, Yakata noted the confusion on his face as he looked at the read-out from the spectrometer.

"What? Something go wrong?"

O'Neal turned toward her, his head shaking. "The test completed before everything shut down, but this doesn't make sense."

She walked over and read the printout:

Processing Error 021:
Spectral Anomaly – Negative Scan

"*Kuso shite shinezo!*" Yakata hissed through clenched teeth.

O'Neal looked at her oddly. "I don't know what you just said, but it sounded painful."

Yakata flushed. Among spacers cursing was one thing, profanity was a part of their make-up. But in front of others, she generally conducted herself more circumspectly. She was just grateful the man did not speak Japanese.

"I apologize for my rudeness. But, damn!" She slammed her hand down on the casing of the machine. "All of that and it's unidentifiable!"

"Not just unidentifiable... it's like nothing's there. The machine didn't even register the walls of the chamber." His expression grew considering. "It's as if the artifact absorbed the light. But to do so this completely... it's impossible for none to have gotten past it."

"Malfunction?"

"Not one I've ever seen, but there's one way to find out."

Captain Kinney had ordered everyone to their stations. But she had to know. She could always double-time it to the command deck.

O'Neal opened the chamber and reached for the artifact. He hissed sharply, as if in pain. His body arched and shuddered.

The look of terror in his eyes sent panic through Yakata. It must be the prosthetic. She remembered the static that had clung to her hand when she'd touched the artifact earlier.

Yakata yanked an equipment bag toward her and rapidly rifled through it. Tucked in the bottom she found a set of insulated gauntlets. She donned them and braced herself against the workstation. With all her weight behind the effort, she hauled on the obelisk until it left his grasp. It came away with the sound of metal scraping metal. Yakata landed in a heap across the compartment, the obelisk heavy on her chest. O'Neal collapsed across the table, greenish static arcing and popping along the length of his arm. He shook his head and groaned. After a moment, he leveled a glare toward Yakata.

Perhaps it was the sparks, or perhaps just the light, but as he stared at her in silence, it seemed his eyes reflected the green hue. He slowly stood and stalked across the room to where she lay. When he reached out his hand, her eyes went wide, expecting pain.

She searched his face for some clue as the man remained silent. His eyes darkened and she couldn't read the swirl of emotions dancing through them. She shivered. He closed his eyes with a sigh. When he opened them all she saw was impatience in their green depth. Green? But...

"The gauntlets..."

She yanked them off and held them up, never taking her eyes from him. He donned the gear and lifted the artifact from her chest. She gasped as breath flooded back into her lungs to full capacity. Damn, that thing was heavy, she swore to herself.

O'Neal turned his back to her. He deposited the obelisk on a metal tray on the table and reinserted the control element he'd used to test the machine initially.

The second reading of the steel bar was identical to the first.

Without a word, Yakata returned the artifact to its storage locker. Using her body as a shield, she keyed the lock with her personal code.

She turned and found O'Neal staring at her. Yakata carefully slipped past him and hurried from the compartment, trying to ignore the faint odor of scorched latex lingering in her nostrils.

PERSONAL LOG ENTRY: 42.05.18 – 1250HRS, DUNN, K.

McKay's systems just flatlined. Everything's back up, but talk about freaking out. What the hell is going on?

Haven't felt like this since I was four and Da took me to the reptile house at the Bronx Zoo. I zoomed all over that place. Couldn't stay still... until I came to the king cobra. Something had pissed it off. It mantled and swayed three feet high in the air, right up close to the glass. It kept up a hiss, low and menacing. Don't know how long I stood there watching its tongue flicker in and out above me, but I couldn't move. Not even when it struck. Lightning-fast it slammed into the glass. To this day, I swear its fangs left long grooves in the surface, dripping with venom.

I still remember the stench of terror. Right now, it's strong in my nose... a hundred times stronger than it was when I was four. And I have that feeling again... like death is hovering above my head and I'm not sure if the glass is going to hold.

Damn... Captain just called duty stations.

COMMAND DECK: 42.05.18 – 1310HRS

Yakata hauled herself through the command deck hatch from the *McKay's* main shaft into a tangible silence. The shaft ran the length of the ship and was fitted out with a ladder that doubled as a track for the slow-moving utility lift. The track could either be climbed or used for crewmen to pull themselves along, depending on the ship's attitude. She had scaled it at record speed, but apparently she hadn't been quick enough.

"First Officer Ushimi... the comm system may have been affected by the anomaly. My order to report to duty stations doesn't seem to have reached all compartments." The captain's words were even and void of tension. His gaze was not. The look he gave her was harder than the artifact she'd left in the lab. "With this sudden glitch, I'm concerned that diagnostics might not show up all malfunctions. I'll need you to conduct an on-site inspection of every comm station and hood on the *McKay*."

Yakata flinched on the inside. "Yes, sir. Right away, sir."

Captain Kinney was known for his swift and fitting discipline. Actually, she'd gotten off easy; she should have been the first on the deck, not counting those who were already there.

There was a sound beneath her feet. She stepped aside to clear the hatch. An acrid aroma preceded Dunn as he clambered to his post.

"Ah, very good." The captain's smile was not very pleasant, though his tone seemed to be. "Crewman Dunn will assist you."

DRIVE SECTION SERVICE MODULE: 42.05.18 – 1700HRS

This was it. The final comm station on her half of the list. Yakata sighed as she pulled out the checklist and ran the last test. Carefully, she removed the housing then used her Fenix utility light and a telescoping mirror to visually inspect the wiring. After that she tested the connections. Finally, she closed the unit and toggled the activator.

"Dunn…"

"Go ahead…"

"Drive section comm inspection complete, how are you coming with the Engineering unit?"

"System's green to go." Dunn's voice remained even but Yakata detected an edge to it. It was barely perceptible, but his breath came out in quick, shallow huffs. She waited for him to report something catastrophic, but he remained silent.

"Okay, that's all of them. Wait for me at the main shaft." Yakata cut the link and toggled the activator again. "Command deck…"

"Go ahead." The captain's voice came through the relay sharp and precise. Yakata winced. He would remain on deck until she relieved him. That was part of what drove home the lesson. Her failure to follow orders affected everyone, right up to the captain, whom she respected more than anyone alive. Nothing, short of a fatality, would have made her feel worse about her lapse in protocol.

"On-site inspection of the communications system complete," Yakata responded, keeping her voice neutral.

"Acknowledged. I'll be waiting to hear your report."

"Yes, sir." Yakata groaned as she cut the link.

With haste, she secured her maintenance kit on her hip, slid the flashlight into its belt loop, and left the compartment. The sensors flanking the door registered her exit. The drive room went dark and the dim, stand-by lights of the causeway brightened. After nearly a decade of service, she generally took the lighting system for granted. Today she newly appreciated the comfort it represented. Even without the recent system's failure, Yakata was uneasy. Her nerves vibrated beneath the surface of her skin and her eyes ached from trying to penetrate the dark spaces around her. She'd yet to spy anything staring back. Her skin crawled though as she imagined a thousand pairs of eyes creeping forward into the now-darkened room behind her. Clenching her teeth, she cocked her head from side to side until the vertebrae ceased to pop. To her left, she thought she heard the faintest sound from somewhere near the pressurized tanks. Probably a loose valve. She made note of the section where she suspected the leak, and set off for the main shaft.

Dunn was not at the rendezvous.

Toggling the activator on her comm hood, the barest edge of anger sharpened her tone. "Crewman Dunn, report..."

Silence.

"Dunn, what is your location?"

Still no response.

What in the world was going on? Their personal comm hoods were the first to be tested. Both had operated fine. She went to the comm screen in the main shaft wall. With a couple of jabs, she input the protocol that instructed the system to display the current location of all crewmembers.

She glanced down the list of names and locations: Captain Kinney and Crewman Suarez—Command deck; Crewmen Jackson and Chapman—Environmental Control Compartment; Specialist O'Neal—Temporary Science Lab; Crewmen Pittman, Jenks, and Gunter—Mess hall; and Crewman Dunn...

Port lateral airlock! Yakata powered down the display and set off back the way she came at a hard clip.

Bad enough they'd both drawn discipline duty, reporting back late would be impossible for the captain to gloss over this time. She tried her comm hood again, activating it with such force she could feel the surrounding fabric pull. "Crewman Dunn... respond..."

Nothing. She put on a little more speed through the shaft. A tight sensation took root in her gut. She tried again, "Come on, Dunn, talk to me. What's going on?"

No answer. The airlocks came into sight. Even in the dim light of the corridor, she could see a dark smear on the floor.

"Dunn! Damnit, Karl! Answer me!"

Yakata closed the last few meters. Dropping to one knee, she touched a finger to the slick spot. It came away bright red, the sweet, metallic tang unmistakable.

What happened? And where was Dunn? Sensors indicated the port airlock, but both chambers were dark. There should be lights. Lighting was automatic. She stepped to the side of the hatch portal and reached for her flashlight. The high-powered beam cut through the black pit beyond the glass.

Yakata gasped. For a second she could do nothing but stand there and stare at the horror revealed by the light: an EVA suit sprawled against the far wall, blood a solid curtain across the faceplate of the helmet.

A burst of static reminded her that the comm hood was still active, on stand-by. The sound snapped her out of the shock.

"Command deck..." She was surprised how low and calm her voice remained. The rest of her trembled. "Command deck, acknowledge..."

The only response was another burst of static.

She moved to the comm unit in the corridor wall and tried again. Again static hissed and crackled through the corridor, echoing through her comm hood. She moved back to the airlock door.

The beam of light glimmered on the helmet like sunlight through rubies. She could make out nothing beyond the faceplate. Swallowing hard, she swept the airlock with light as far as she could from side to side. Nothing. Not even more smears. No movement. Still, something did this. Yakata was acutely aware of the blind spots to either side of the hatch.

She punched in the sequence to open the airlock. The keypad didn't respond. She tightened her grip on the flashlight. It was awkward manipulating the manual release one-handed, but, with determination, she managed it. The hatch opened smoothly. Out wafted the heavy, copper-penny scent of blood and something else, something bitter and sharp. The lights still didn't engage.

"Dunn, can you respond?"

She peered into the room, her head just past the collar as she flashed the light into the corner to the right of the door. Nothing.

As she brought her light around to the other side, the comm hood gave a more energetic hiss. She flinched back at the unexpected sound. A blur of motion from the left caught her eye. Metal slammed against metal. From the shadows, hoarse breathing punched up into a roar. She now recognized the acrid odor in the air. She'd smelt it on the command deck, when Dunn came up the hatch.

There wasn't time to call out to him. There was only time to move. An industrial-grade spanner crashed into the airlock door just millimeters away from her head. Again, the weapon rose. She couldn't continue to evade; not in this restricted space. She brought the utility light up to block the spanner's descent and allowed her body to fall back upon the deck. The move cost her the light, which went spinning away, but her bones were intact.

She stared up into Dunn's face. He was barely recognizable. His eyes were wide and wild, a long, bloody scratch marred his face, and sweat stood out in hard beads on his forehead. The rest of him was coated in blood. He did not seem to recognize her. She watched as a tremor ran through his body. No matter what had passed between them, she didn't want to hurt him, not even to get away. She would, but she didn't want to. She prayed he came out of it.

"Dunn... Karl, what happened to you?"

She held her breath. For a moment, his pupils expanded. Recognition floated just beneath the surface. Then her comm hood hissed. His echoed in response. She had most of a second to watch him retreat behind the terror.

"Oh shit!" Yakata braced herself. This was going to hurt. Her only hope lay in the leverage of her position and her greater lower-body strength. The spanner came down full force. She dodged her torso as best she could, but took a glancing blow to her shoulder. Her left side went numb on impact. She wrapped herself around the spanner with her good arm and drew her legs up sharp. Snarling, she planted both feet in Dunn's gut and shoved for all she was worth.

The weapon remained in her possession, though it was close. Dunn went flying. Yakata winced as he crashed into the lockers, landing awkwardly on the sprawled EVA suit. She bit her lip at the fresh smear of blood across the dented metal. Bit harder against the impulse to go to him. Instead, she rolled to her feet and slammed the airlock hatch. Using the spanner, she wedged the door closed as best she could. It wouldn't hold long. She headed for the main shaft at a hard clip. Within the first five strides, the pain in her left arm triggered a grey haze across her vision. Gasping, she stopped running immediately.

Yakata blinked furiously, forcing herself to take slow, deep breaths, until the haze went away. Behind her she could hear banging, enraged and violent.

Gritting her teeth against the pain, she loosened her web belt and slipped the wrist of her damaged arm into the gap between belt and pants, angled across her stomach. She hissed with the pain and the sounds from the airlock increased in intensity.

She forced Dunn out of her thoughts and tightened the belt against her wrist, immobilizing the damaged arm as best she could. Once again, she set off, this time at a gentler, swinging lope. Her gut clenched. As she left the cacophony of the drive section behind, the faint sound of a warning klaxon could be heard elsewhere on the ship.

Yakata toggled her comm activator again. "Command deck... Come in, Captain Kinney." Not even a hiss sounded in her ear. "Deck officer, respond."

No answer; and her comm went dead, completely dead.

Abandoning her gentle pace, Yakata ran full out for the transport. The lift was slow, but one-handed, she would be even slower hauling herself up the ladder to the command deck. Her eyes locked on the lift mooring as it came into sight. The knots in her shoulders eased the slightest increment. The platform was there. She added another burst of speed.

Her steps faltered as she drew close. Something was not right. The lift wasn't seated properly in the track. It hovered about six inches off the mooring. She stopped where she was and tried to peer beneath it.

How had she missed the thin, crimson rivulets snaking across the deck? The fine, meandering tributaries flowing from the crushed body of Crewman Dave Jackson? Yakata fought the urge to be sick.

Was Dunn responsible? Was this why he wasn't at the rendezvous? Why he didn't answer her hails? Her throat spasmed and she had to swallow hard as she moved closer to examine the mechanism.

The body was tangled in the power couplings, bits of it pulped by the gears. Even if she could get the lift into motion, it would shred what was left of him. Only his face was untouched. His expression would haunt her.

A sound echoed up the corridor. Cursing, Yakata re-tightened her belt against her injured arm and climbed onto the lift. Her added force caused the platform to drop another inch. There was a sickening crack as something organic gave. She clenched her teeth and closed her eyes, emptied her mind of everything, and started up the lift. Before it had gone more than a few meters she slumped to her knees.

Central Shaft, Upper Utility Lift Mooring: 42.05.18 – 2100hrs

The lift locked into its upper mooring. Before her was the command deck hatch. She should get up. She had to report. The captain was waiting for them. Them. Not just her. Reality came rushing back. Yakata yanked herself to her feet with her good arm and gripped the ladder-track for balance. The hatch was open and the deck lights were at standby dim.

Every nerve in her body pricked. The command deck was unmanned. It was never unmanned. Leaning into the ladder, Yakata braced herself. She released her grip with her good hand and reached down into her maintenance kit. Near the bottom, she found the telescoping mirror she'd used earlier. Taking the reflective end carefully between her teeth, she angled the head and drew out the handle as far as it would go. She then edged the tool around the hatch. There were no bodies on the deck, and there were none walking around, either. Not that she could see, anyway.

The lights flared higher as she pulled herself through the hatch. She squinted against the sudden brilliance. It took a moment for her eyes to adjust. Closing the hatch, she keyed the lock with her personal code. Dunn wouldn't corner her again. Her shoulder throbbed in agreement. With a grimace, she settled into the command chair. Multiple warnings lit up the display in front of her. Alerts flashed over nearly every inch of the ship, a confusing dance of flood, fire, and vacuum. Sometimes all three at once in the same compartment. How much of it was real?

Clearing the screen, she prayed nothing would go critical before she could get this sorted out. She ran diagnostics, keying in commands one-handed. Half of the alerts disappeared. Next, she toggled the comm on the console. Nothing. Not even static. She had to try, though.

"Yakata to all crew, report." She set the hail to repeat and went back to diagnostics. It was halfway through and there were no major malfunctions yet. A host of minor ones, but those they could survive. Of course, that assumed the diagnostics system wasn't fried as well.

She then input the command to identify the locations of all on board, just as she had when she looked for Dunn. It took longer this time. The computer spit out multiple conflicting responses. There was no way to tell which one was accurate.

While she waited for diagnostics to complete, Yakata moved to the emergency kit. She selected an analgesic patch. After tearing it open with her teeth, she palmed it and slipped it past the collar of her coverall. It was cool, instantly soothing her battered shoulder. That taken care of, she settled back into the command chair.

Diagnostics was at ninety-five percent. Another alert went off as the logarithm completed. Yakata's eyes moved from the diagnostics display to the main console. It was the proximity warning. It shouldn't have gone off when they were under hyperdrive. She stood and went to the external monitoring station. Nothing appeared on the fore view. Yakata activated the aft cameras. Her finger trembled as she depressed the button. Her vision greyed out one moment, only to telescope into sharp focus the next. Something drifted by the lens out by the drive section, caught in the electromagnetic pocket of e'space surrounding the ship. Several somethings, in fact. Yakata swallowed against the acidic tang climbing her throat. Visions of her father's helmet overwhelmed her, eclipsing the images she didn't want to see. She distanced herself through extreme willpower and zoomed in on the debris.

"...all crew, report."

"Shit!" Yakata yelled as her own voice suddenly called out through both her comm hood and every speaker on the deck. Communications was back. She killed the auto repeat and sent out a fresh hail.

"Command deck to Captain Kinney..."

Her voice trailed off as she tweaked the settings on the monitor. The objects had come into focus. Her eyes slammed closed. But even with them tightly shut she could still see the empty gaze of Captain Kinney staring at her from the vacuum of space.

PERSONAL LOG ENTRY: 42.05.18 – 2230HRS, DUNN, K.

FUCK YOU! I don't know what you are, but I know what you're doing now, so fuck you! You made me hurt her. I would never hurt her. She is the only one who cares. Who still means something to me...

I know you can access what I'm writing here, because you knew how to mess with my head. Well access this: You will NEVER get me to hurt her again. You will never touch her again. I will destroy you!

DUTY LOG: 42.05.19 – 1230HRS, YAKATA, U.

Reactor status – indeterminate;
O_2 levels – fluctuating;
Power – data unavailable.

Note: SC McKay operating under emergency conditions. Ship-wide malfunctions worsen. Member or members of the crew unstable. Captain Kinney; deceased, means unknown, body expelled from ship by unidentified personnel. At least three others likewise expelled, positive id cannot be made. Crewman Chapman; deceased, accidental or by design. Crewman Dunn; unstable, violent, temporarily restrained in port lateral airlock. Remainder of the crew; status unknown. First Officer Ushimi Yakata assuming command.

Out of habit, Yakata printed a hard copy of the duty log. Events must always be documented. Not that she expected anyone would ever read this account. As she tore the sheet from the printer, her eyes drifted across the page. She cursed and jerked her hand away. The page drifted to the deck, bold, black letters stared up at her:

They're all dead. You're all dead. Die already, bitch.

There was the faintest of sounds behind her. She whirled. O'Neal came through the hatch across the command deck, the one leading to the cargo bay and rendezvous station.

She took in the metallurgist's appearance: his coverall was torn, and dark stains across his chest glistened wetly. There was no sign he was the party injured. At his side, his prosthetic arm slowly flexed, as if the motion were unconscious. Yakata met O'Neal's gaze. She did not recognize the man staring back at her. His eyes were cold and hard, alien and bereft of humanity. His expression was neutral; as if she wouldn't notice something else lurked beneath. *There was so much wrong with this picture,* Yakata thought fleetingly.

"You plan to do what you're told?" he asked in a slow drawl, nodding toward the slip of acrylisheet on the floor.

His tone sounded as flat as his expression. Yakata's eyes flickered to the printout.

"I don't take orders from a piece of paper," she growled. "And I sure as hell don't take orders from you."

"We all have to answer to someone."

"Yeah, well the only person I answered to is drifting out by the engines," Yakata spat back at him. "Who do you answer to?" She moved to the side as she spoke, edging toward the hatch.

"You'll meet soon enough." The neutrality was gone. Pure evil crept through O'Neal's voice. He followed her movements like a raptor tracking prey.

Forget that, Yakata told herself. With the line of her body to block the action, she lowered her right hand back into her maintenance kit. Very carefully, she eased out her utility knife, her hand through the wrist strap and the hilt solid in her palm. She depressed the release button on the pommel and the blade silently deployed.

Yakata's muscles rippled beneath her skin. She braced herself, poised to react to whatever move O'Neal made. Her only real option was evasion. If he got a hold of her with that prosthetic, he would crush her before she could even flinch.

As the metallurgist advanced, a tremor went straight through Yakata's body. It took her a moment to realize it wasn't internal. She sucked in a sharp breath. Her gaze flickered away from O'Neal to the main display. Alert icons flashed, one by one. The system was losing power. Within moments they would no longer have enough to sustain hyperdrive. There was a boot dock just behind her and a tether up and to her right. She was going to need one of them shortly.

It would have to be the boot dock; she had too few functioning hands to grab a tether and use the knife. She edged herself closer. Let him think she was afraid of him; that she futilely distanced herself.

She was ready when the bottom dropped out of the universe. The ship shuddered as the electrogravitic drive envelope disintegrated. Simultaneously, she leaned back and jammed her heel into the dock. She was barely secure when there was a pop and a flash as intense as a hundred strobes going off right there in the room. Yakata squeezed her eyes shut just in time. From the heaving sounds, O'Neal had been caught unaware. She opened her eyes as reality righted itself in an orbital orientation. O'Neal floated in an uncontrolled sprawl on the far side of the command console. Around him floated globes of acrid vomit. As he bumped them, they burst into a dozen smaller globes, minus what clung to him. Feebly, his hand reached for the edge of the console.

Yakata grinned. In this state, he was no threat at all.

He groaned, and she laughed. She couldn't help it.

She went somber quickly, though, as hatred sharpened his gaze. The stench of malevolence overpowered the odor of bile. He looked ready to launch at her. Yakata tightened her grip on the utility knife. Let him try. He was a ground-pounder. Space was her element, and this was her ship.

There was a clunk and the manual release on the command deck hatch spun toward open. Yakata froze. Once she'd keyed the lock, even the manual release required her personal code to open the hatch. Only one person onboard had the slightest chance of figuring it out. Dunn.

Confusion infiltrated the evil glint in O'Neal's eye. She watched fury flood his expression as the hatch swung out. The open portal remained empty.

Yakata didn't relax. Now she had to be on her guard on two fronts, and her ex was no rookie in space. He must have been the one to disable the drive system. He certainly had the knowledge.

"Don't just stand there, 'Ta!"

Dunn peered around the edge of the hatch as he snapped at her. The scratch across his face had crusted over. His expression danced between violence and panic. She shifted her grip on the utility knife and turned her body so that her good arm could strike at either O'Neal or Dunn.

From the far side of the command console, O'Neal let out a serpentine hiss. She resisted the urge to turn to stare at him. Dunn represented the more potent threat at the moment.

She watched the muscles of his face clench and twitch in response to the sound O'Neal made. Dunn's breath quickened. The massive spanner he'd used earlier came into view. She braced herself, ready to yank her heel out of the dock the second she knew which direction to propel herself. But his attention wasn't on her. Dunn's eyes locked with O'Neal's. Yakata's gaze flickered from one to the other. Between them, they blocked the only ways out.

"Will you move it before he figures out how to get both of us!"

Yakata jumped, startled as Dunn spoke in rapid Japanese. She'd forgotten he knew her language. It wasn't something they'd used often. They both knew that O'Neal didn't share their knowledge. The entire crew was required to familiarize themselves with his profile before he came on board. She was surprised Dunn had enough of a grip on himself to use that intel.

"What... and I'm supposed to trust you over him?" She slashed back in the same tongue. "He's not the one who tried to cave in my head!"

"Just move it, 'Ta!" Dunn continued in Japanese. Sweat gleamed on his forehead and his eyes were wild.

Before she could dodge aside, he lunged. His free hand latched onto her belt. She snarled as he jerked her loose from the dock. Yakata gasped with pain, her damaged arm wrenched about by his handling. Her head spun at the sharp, sudden movement. Dunn angled her toward the hatch with practiced ease. At the same time, the hand gripping the spanner swung out, aimed at O'Neal's head.

There was a solid *thunk*: the sound of metal against flesh. Silence followed. Threat floated thick on the canned air. Yakata shifted her head to look back at O'Neal. His green eyes glowed with malice. She cursed and lost the thought as her quick glance took in his unbloodied head and Dunn's spanner caught by the metallurgist's flesh hand. Some oddly detached part of her brain wondered why he hadn't just grabbed it with the prosthetic.

Her answer was a strangled gasp from Dunn. With no visible effort, O'Neal's cybernetic limb crushed Dunn's wrist, the one holding the spanner.

The sight refocused Yakata's rage in an instant. She tried to wrench away from Karl's grip, throwing herself back as far as his tethering hold allowed to slash at his attacker with her utility knife. The tip sliced through O'Neal's shirt, barely scratching his shoulder. He did not even flinch.

Her curses cut off abruptly as Dunn shook her hard.

"Go! Now!" Karl snapped. Pain glimmered in his eyes, brilliant and jagged. Beneath that, he wordlessly pled with her. She stopped struggling, her brow drawn down in confusion.

Executing an effortless turn, she used the tip of her toe to propel herself off the overhead toward the hatch. She torpedoed through the opening, dropped the utility knife to hang by its strap, and caught the hatch collar with her good hand. Behind her a sick grinding sound filled the command deck.

She pivoted, catching sight of Dunn on his knees, his captured arm bent impossibly high behind his back. She growled and started to return to the command deck. She couldn't leave him to this.

"No! I said go! One of us has to get away... head for the Cans, now!" Despite his obvious pain, he continued speaking in Japanese. Yakata hissed in objection, but she dipped her head in a brief, sharp nod before pivoting around to zip down the main shaft. Behind her, she heard a loud snap as the sick sound of laughter drifted through the hatch. She had to fight the impulse to turn around and tear O'Neal to shreds.

"Yes... do run, little rabbit... I'll be along as soon as I'm done here. Shouldn't take long."

Yakata's blood thickened and her heart froze. O'Neal had just spoken to her in flawless, textbook Japanese.

An agonized scream came from the command deck. It rose sharply before an abrupt end.

Her good arm burned nearly as bad as her injured one. She ignored it and grabbed another rung of the ladder-track, slingshoting herself down the shaft. The echo of Dunn's final scream followed her. It filled her head until she heard nothing else. She tried to force the memory into the fading recesses where it belonged. It resisted.

The flickers of movement were back. The flashes of light behind her, just to the side of her vision. Halfway down the shaft it got to her. Growling deep in her throat, she turned to confront the phantoms that stalked her. A practiced flick of her wrist sent the utility knife back up into her grip and a moment's pressure deployed the blade. Her momentum sent her colliding with the substructure. The impact to her damaged arm sent true sparks across her vision, followed by a grey haze. She blinked it away and cursed.

The shaft behind her was empty. There was nothing behind her, and nowhere anyone might hide. She retracted the knife and let it drift at the end of its strap. With a little more care, she turned and continued to haul herself along, both arms throbbing as she went.

Her comm hood gave a sudden burst of static. Yakata jumped. Another growl filled her throat pulsing against her jaw.

She nearly snatched the comm hood off to shred the delicate wiring.

"What the hell are you doing?!"

The unexpected outburst stayed her hand. Dunn. How...? Her gaze snapped to the command deck many stories above her head. She couldn't see him. He must be watching her on the monitors.

"I told you... to get out of here! Get to the Cans... now!" Dunn's voice was thin, strained.

"What happened to O'Neal?"

"Don't know... I passed out. He's not here." Sounds of movement filtered through the comm; rustling, a sharply drawn breath. What might have been a strangled sob...

"Dunn? Dunn!" Yakata's suspicions disintegrated beneath a fresh wave of concern.

"Don't yell, 'Ta." Karl's voice was low and weak. "You're making it hard to think.

"He left me for dead, which means he's after you."

"I don't understand what's going on here," she whispered.

"It's that damn artifact," he snapped back, but his voice quickly faded, slurring and losing focus. "None of this started until we salvaged that thing. It's screwing with our minds. It's screwing with the ship. Somehow it's infiltrated the system... and..." Static disrupted him in sharp bursts. "...anything elec-tronic ...nly use manual overr... only. Not malfunc... deliberate."

"The artifact! I have to get the artifact!"

"No! ...amnit! Get the hell off this ship. Now!"

Immediately, uncertainty sank firm fingers into her thoughts. She had more reason to doubt Dunn than to trust him. And O'Neal had already proven their attempt at speaking covertly had failed.

"Move!"

No. Perhaps O'Neal left him for dead... or not. Dunn had attacked her once already. She couldn't help but wonder if this was a trap.

She would get her artifact, and then she was getting off this ship. It was foolhardy to continue to the airlocks, though. That's where they expected her to go. Besides, the Cans—as the escape pods were called by any spacer with experience—had precious little reserve, and almost no maneuverability. The distress signal was a joke. She wasn't ditching this ship just to suffocate slowly in space.

Like a swimmer doing laps, Yakata flipped end over end and hauled herself the way she'd come. The pods weren't the only option. There was that payload attached to the forward coupling, the inter-orbital shuttlecraft meant to transport Corporate bigwigs to their facilities surrounding Demeter. Even if O'Neal knew about it, he wouldn't expect her to try and escape that way. Transports were shipped dry, no fuel, no external tanks, and just enough juice to power the maneuvering thrusters and internals. Right now the shuttle was a big, floating box. But— most important for her—that big, floating box contained enough air to support seven adult males for fourteen days, without cracking the reserve tanks. That... and a state-of-the-art distress beacon.

All she had to do was reach it. Yakata renewed her efforts, keeping her eye on the reflectors as she went. No one threatened to come through the hatches ahead of her. As she neared the Temporary Science Lab, she again glanced both ways down the shaft.

Wherever O'Neal had gone, he wasn't stalking her.

Yakata opened the compartment and dove inside. She thanked God that the drive had not reengaged. The only blessing in this whole thing: weightlessness certainly made it easy to get around. Not to mention the obelisk would have been a dead weight if the ship were still under gravity.

Lights flared as Yakata slipped into the section where the artifact was stored. Immediately she noticed the door to the locker hung open, and nothing remained inside.

"No!" Yakata hissed with rage. She looked around, her gaze darting frantically, as if the obelisk might be sitting right in front of her. But it was useless. It was gone. She slammed the locker door and whirled, her anger taking over. The spectrometer still sat affixed to the table. It mocked her. She'd known O'Neal was out to screw her over. Her good hand snapped out, denting the housing of his costly machine. She let it fly again. It felt good. She took aim once more, until a reflection in the battered metal caught her eye.

O'Neal! She dove away from his raised fists, certain that any moment she would feel the crushing blow from his prosthetic. None fell. She twisted in midair, fighting to control her motions, to palm her knife and deploy the blade.

As she came to rest against the far bulkhead, Yakata felt a ripple of laughter seize her throat.

"What the hell?" she murmured aloud. The room was empty. No, O'Neal hovered, ready to pummel her to pulp. Yet...

Yakata gripped her knife tighter and propelled herself toward the spectrometer. Had she truly lost it? Or was this proof of the sinister force Dunn claimed now possessed the ship? She tapped the dented surface with the tip of her utility knife. Tapped it right over the reflection of O'Neal. The micro image flinched back. Yakata giggled. It sounded jagged.

That was it then: she'd gone over the edge. She giggled again and chased the figmentary O'Neal around the spectrometer with rapid taps of her utility knife. She laughed full out and tasted salt drip over the rim of her lip onto her tongue. A sob slipped out next. The knife drifted down to its strap and she rested a gentle hand against the reflection.

"I'm sorry... I'm so sorry..."

She brought her face right up near the metal, noticing the terror on that tiny man's face. He wasn't looking at her, though; his gaze stared off into the room. It took her a moment to realize there were now two O'Neals trapped in the metal. Perhaps it was an accumulative thing: the longer she stared the more the image would multiply. Her next giggle bordered on a wail.

That was when the *ching* of flexing metal reached her ears. Her eyes went wide. She leaned against the machine. Clarity seeped back into her own reflection. The memory of the last time she and O'Neal had been in this room came to her. He'd taken the artifact out of the spectrometer and gone into painful convulsions. Her gaze snapped to the tiny O'Neal with the hazel eyes, somehow trapped within his own machine while something went around in his body. He gave the slightest nod. "I am sorry," she whispered as she snaked her hand around the housing.

With a mighty heave, she flung the machine at the O'Neal creeping up behind her, the one with something alien peering out of stormy green eyes.

Power couplings snapped. Metal collided with metal in a satisfying crunch. The creature's roar deafened her.

As she rocketed past, aiming for the hatch, she spared half a glance for her would-be attacker. The spectrometer drifted away from him. Massive bruises shadowed O'Neal's already dark shoulder. The prosthetic attached to it was crumpled, but the fingers flexed, if somewhat haltingly.

Her aim was off. She'd meant to cave in his head.

There was an odd gleam in O'Neal's eye as he locked gazes with her. She jerked her eyes away and maneuvered out of arm's reach.

She was nearly clear when he lurched up. His flesh hand shot out and grabbed her ankle. Screaming with rage, she flicked her wrist and palmed the dangling utility knife, the blade still deployed. She lashed out. The edge bit deep into the back of his hand.

She jerked the knife free and kicked out with her unfettered foot at O'Neal's still firm and bloodied grip on her ankle. He laughed up at her. The trapped O'Neal pounded furiously from the far side of his reflection; the evil one raised his battered prosthetic and caressed her calf with deceptive gentleness.

Frantic, Yakata tried to yank her foot free. She succeeded only in drawing him closer. Again the prosthetic stroked her leg, this time higher.

"Shh... It'll be okay..." he mocked.

Her vision went dark and flat. Nothing had depth or shading. Nothing was as crisply clear as his grip on her leg. Nothing mattered more than freeing herself from that hold. Without a second thought, she brought her knife around again and impaled O'Neal's hand...

...straight through to her ankle. More blood filled the room.

"Augh!"

O'Neal laughed over her scream as he tugged his hand away from the blade, bisecting his own flesh. The damage did nothing to hinder his movements. But for her, the motion sent shafts of breath-stopping pain shooting from her foot to the top of her head. The knife remained lodged in the muscle just above the ankle.

"Bad girl... you were supposed to head for the Cans."

Yakata whimpered. Clenching her teeth, she yanked out the blade, sending pearls of blood spinning through the bay. The strap went back over her wrist. The hilt locked in her grip. Again armed, she kicked off toward the hatch.

From just inside the room, O'Neal's laughter stole her breath. She waited for him to haul her back. She could already feel his fingers locked around her. Not again! She sent herself rocketing forward with reckless force. Her body careened off the interior walls. She slammed against the hatch collar with her bad shoulder. The injured foot snagged on the door. Agony nearly crippled her as her vision clouded and a buzz filled her ears.

It wasn't enough to drown out O'Neal as he called after her. "Run, little rabbit, run... it's so much fun to catch you."

Despite O'Neal's taunt, there were no sounds of pursuit. She had no illusion it would remain that way. Tumbling into the main shaft, Yakata planted her good foot against the track and shoved off, bulleting toward the nose of the ship. She cursed at the lights. Some sections activated as she passed, others went out, plunging her into darkness. She ignored it. After all her years on this ship, a little darkness wasn't going to screw her up.

As she neared the command deck there was a faint green ambient glow, like that given off by digital displays in the dark. It was impossible to make out if anyone was there. O'Neal was somewhere behind her, but what happened to Dunn? Intense sorrow gripped her heart as she remembered the last time she saw him. Yakata forced it away. He was either dead, or a danger to her.

Cautiously, she eased past the command hatch, keeping to the far side of the shaft. It was slow going, but she made it to the staging bay two levels up without incident. A glance behind her revealed no obvious motion, but her nerves vibrated with tension.

She turned back to the open hatch of the staging bay. The mechanism to seal the two-meter wide opening could close in less than thirty seconds. She released the knife and reached into her pouch for a spanner, wedging it into the grating where the retractable hatch was housed. It wouldn't hold long, but should another... malfunction occur, the obstruction would give her a little extra time to get clear.

Reaching just past the opening, she felt around for a tether bar to haul herself through. Something brushed against her hand in the darkness. She jerked back and palmed the knife, bracing herself for an attack. A whisper of sound taunted her ears. Her grip on the knife tightened even more, but nothing else came at her out of the dark. Yakata breathed out a growl.

Fine, she thought. *I'll do it the hard way.* She flung herself through the hatch, rocketing past the opening and deep into the bay, her body angled to intersect with the lift track. Instead, she collided with something soft and yielding. It was impossible not to scream as arms came around to encircle her.

No! She would not be caught so easily! Yakata brought up her knife and thrust brutally into the one blocking her way.

"'Ta...'" The whisper was faint, and right by her ear. Yakata moaned and her knife hand jerked back. Warm globules bounced against her skin as the blade did more damage coming out than going in. The pinpoints of warmth sent her trembling.

No! Oh, God, no! Please no! Yakata's thoughts were frantic. She released the knife as if it were a contagion. Her now-empty hand scrambled around in her maintenance pouch as the knife bobbed on its strap. *Where was it? Where, damnit?* She forgot all about escape as she searched for her spare light among the jumbled tools. As her hand wrapped around it, and she depressed the button, a sudden clang from the direction of the hatch startled her. She fumbled the light. It made eerie arcs as it spun in the darkened bay, revealing small slices of her surroundings. Her gasp echoed through the compartment as the rotating beam briefly illuminated a blood-coated hand. Yakata lunged for the maintenance light. Before she could bring the beam around, there was a deep, rumbling chuckle behind her. She whirled and the main lights flared to life in the bay. She flinched and squinted against the sudden brilliance.

"My... and haven't you been busy?" O'Neal rested against the lift track, his arms crossed over his chest as he watched her. She noticed his gaze sweep the chamber. He frowned faintly as he looked right, but he made no move toward her or the room.

The last thing she should do was take her eyes off him. The impulse, however, was irresistible. Yakata pivoted until she could see the whole of the bay.

The blood rushed from her head. She barely heard O'Neal's malicious laughter. Around her floated three bodies. Her unaccounted-for crewmen... She immediately recognized the one to the right as Dunn, much bloodier, but still clearly him. The closest to her, however, was John Pittman. From his gut streamed a trail of ruby-red bubbles.

She was overcome by the urge to fling the utility knife from her, only that would have cut her probability of survival down even lower. It was an effort to tug her eyes away, to get past the horror. She told herself he was already dead. Beyond Pittman floated Anita Suarez, her expression softer, more feminine in death than it had ever been in life. Old spacer that she was, she looked like a frightened child now. A frightened child frozen in intense and unbearable pain.

Yakata refused to look more closely at Dunn.

She cursed and turned on O'Neal once more, her knife in her hand, though she didn't remember flicking it up. O'Neal continued to laugh.

"'Ta... no..."

Again, the bodiless whisper by her ear. No... from her comm hood! Only Dunn ever call her 'Ta. She glanced sideways, trying to catch the subtle motion breathing alone would have caused. It was so hard to tell at this angle.

"Damn it, 'Ta, come... get this thing..." The strained whisper was no product of her imagination. He 'drifted' ever so slightly; just enough to reveal the outline of a line-gun hidden in the curve of his body. Behind him she could see the half-open storage locker the tool had come from.

Without another thought, she braced both legs against the wall. Pain rippled from her ankle, but she needed equal force to keep herself headed straight as she launched herself forward. O'Neal arrowed toward Dunn, as well, but Yakata was closer.

Grasping the gun and using her momentum to pivot the rest of her mass, she braced the improvised weapon against her body and jerked the release.

There was a *whoosh* and a *thud*. O'Neal went rocketing across the bay toward the opposite wall. His head slammed into the hull and then the only motion was his body recoiling from the impact.

Numbness set in. *Could that be it? Was it that simple?* she thought as she drifted where she was, the gun still gripped in her hand. Beside her, Dunn moaned and it barely reached where her psyche had retreated.

The steady tug on the rope, though... that went right to her nerve centers.

"Oh, shit!" She let go of the line-gun and wrapped her good hand in Dunn's vest.

"N-no... you have to survive," he murmured, batting away her hand. "Can't do that hauling my ass behind you."

"Bullshit!" she growled. "You made it this far, I'm not leaving you here to die."

"I'm... I'm d-dead, either way."

She ignored his failing whisper, and pushed off, sending them past the bodies. Her mind shut down as she did so, focused on one goal: freedom. Nothing existed but the nose dock of the *McKay* and the payload it led to.

And suddenly, they were there.

She let go of Dunn's vest to work the manual release. The hatch clanged open and she reached for Dunn once more. He gripped her hand back. He trembled violently. She turned to look at him, to gauge how much distress he was in.

"No!" she shouted, as she spied O'Neal past Dunn's shoulder, raising the retracted line-gun. But it was too late. She felt the impact as the hook embedded itself in Karl's back. "No... no..." she sobbed. Not Dunn. Not when she... "No... I l-love you! No!"

Tears streamed down her face as she watched the awareness fade from his eyes. *No.* But this protest was silent, weak. *Does it matter now,* she wondered, *if I get away?* But the tug of the line decided her. She roared with rage and yanked back. O'Neal and whatever rode him would not have Dunn.

She brought up her utility knife and severed the line. Grabbing Karl's vest, she tugged him through the forward airlock. He bobbed behind her as she cycled the hatch. Yakata was numb as she took them through the yacht access. She gave him a gentle nudge to send him drifting deeper into the cabin as her hand danced automatically through the manual release sequence for the docking ring.

As they separated from the *McKay*, she could swear she heard the ghost of O'Neal's laughter.

She dropped into the command chair of the luxury yacht, barely noticing the sensual caress of fine doeskin leather. Her only concern was powering up the systems. Lighting and atmospherics engaged, followed by the exterior cameras.

The numbness faded as she realized how near Demeter they were. There was hope of rescue. A solid chance for survival. Her hand hovered over the distress beacon, but drew back, leaving the unit inactivated. Why bother? Dunn was gone.

"No... you must survive."

Yakata shivered as Dunn's earlier words whispered through her thoughts. Clenching her eyes against the heartache, she brought her hand back and slammed it down on the distress beacon button.

Rescue would come now. And she would have to go on. Alone.

As that realization hit her, she watched the *McKay* fire its engines. She deftly manipulated the contoured joystick controlling the external camera, panning it in the ship's wake.

What is he up to now? she wondered, unable to turn away. The *McKay* angled further to the left and the display in front of her blazed fiercely, blinding her a moment. The system adjusted the filters until the brilliant sun was no more than a distant, glowing disk marred only by a rapidly diminishing black speck.

"Enjoying the show, Ms. Ushimi?"

Yakata jerked as O'Neal's voice came over the yacht's speakers. She cursed herself for forgetting to disengage the remote sensors connecting the two ships.

"Why?" she hissed.

"Where's the terror," he purred, "if there's no one left to know exactly how fucked you all are?

"Oh yes, and thanks for the ride."

As his words faded, the yacht's lights flickered out, plunging Yakata into darkness. She fumbled with the control panel, frantically trying to reengage them, to no avail. Her only illumination was the display in front of her.

She couldn't hold back a whimper. She was no longer comfortable with the dark. O'Neal's disembodied laugh wrapped around her just before he closed the link. She was so shocked it took a moment for her to realize the McKay's hyperdrive had engaged.

Horrified, she watched the ship's graceful arc; the shimmer of its electrogravitic drive envelope mesmerized her. Yakata held her breath. She could still see the glittering trail streaming behind the transport, but knew it had, in fact, already plunged into the sun. Eight minutes later, the sunlight contracted, the glowing ball getting smaller and smaller.

O'Neal's voice echoed in her head. An old memory from when he had still been himself and the spectrometer had fed them an impossible reading on the obelisk: *It's as if the artifact absorbed the light.*

She shuddered and watched as the star died, its fire eaten up by an ancient evil no larger than her head.

Yakata found herself in complete darkness with her dead.

Dunn. The spaced crew. In her panicked mind, she pictured each of them in a mask of her father's face.

Her breath came in rapid huffs and her body shook until she had to grip the console to remain in the chair.

How long before we all die? she thought, staring in the direction of Demeter, an entire planet suddenly and inexplicably plunged into bitter-cold darkness.

The comm hood crackled and Yakata's heart seized.

"Yummy," O'Neal's voice whispered malevolently in her ear. "Want to come get us? We'll do dessert..."

Yakata screamed.

Burning Conviction

ULTRAFINE. INSIDIOUS. SOFTLY SUFFOCATING. FINE, CLINGING DUST coated the cavernous chamber and everything in it. It rose in swirling puffs with every step I took. I rubbed my fingertips together and flinched. The dust clung in persistent defiance of any efforts to slough it off. The powder mocked me with a phantom glide of natural oil that spoke of past incarnations. Sweat beaded on my forehead and streamed into my eyes. More trickled between my breasts and down the rest of me. It mingled with the dust that permeated everything I was wearing. Soon I would resemble the troll-like men moving about the chamber. They were coated in a thick grey crust that cracked, but never seemed to fall away.

Across the room an entire wall of massive convection ovens roared. As I moved closer, the infernal heat drew everything from the air—dust... humidity... oxygen. I opened my mouth to suck in what was to be had. The air scorched my lungs. The heat stole my body's moisture as I choked on dust.

"Someone get this fuckin' log outa my way until I'm ready for it!"

I tensed as the troll shoved past me.

"Stack it over with the others...now!"

I cocked an eye in the direction he gestured to with his thick, knobby chin. Piled longwise in the shadows were disturbingly familiar bundles, each between five and six feet long. Black bound in a fabric that glimmered with a dull sheen, there was a rough symmetry to them—small and rounded at the top, then doubling in thickness, until they tapered to a blunt point—but no two were exact in length or size. I quickly turned away. My jaw clenched and I swallowed hard against the sensation tightening my throat. A snarl twitched my lips. I lunged forward.

"Move me yourself, you ugly fucker!" I screamed back at him. "Who are you calling a…" An explosive pop sounded from the oven, cutting me off. White-hot flames shot out the opening.

The man didn't even look at me. He gave no sign that he heard my words. Instead, troll boy yelled and cursed and hurried toward the gapping maw of the blazing oven. Granite arms came around my chest and another set caught up my legs. I struggled and fought like a demon, screaming and cursing to rival the man in charge. He continued to ignore me as he grabbed a massive, charred paddle from the corner and slammed it into the fire. There was a loud crack, like bones breaking, and the sound of steam escaping. It rose with the eerie cadence of a keen. I shivered at the suffering in that sound; fell still and silent at the disturbing look on the man's face as he slid the paddle beneath the mound he'd just pummeled and flipped the mass over within the flame. A piece fell free.

I went limp in the grip of those carrying me. Tremors shook my body and my stomach heaved as I stared at the black, gnarled lump that landed just at the edge of the flame. My mind shut down, refusing to recognize what it saw. But it was too late for denial: there before me lay a disembodied hand, black and frozen in a frantic, useless claw.

"Okay. I'm ready," he grunted, shoving the paddle aside.

Those hauling me toward the mound stopped, and instead moved me forward.

I felt the fire's heat upon my face and screamed.

PURGATORY

*Purgatory is when
something inside of you
is certain you've been damned.
Hell is when it's right.*

HEAT... SUFFOCATING HEAT... I CANNOT BREATHE. MY CHEST HEAVES and my hands claw frantically. I am burning up and I cannot fight free. Visions of fire crowd my panic-stricken mind. Vibrant flames paint the darkness behind my eyes while the stench of burning human hair weaves past my nostrils. I feel the whimper before I hear the muffled scream. It takes a moment to realize both come from me.

Harsher shrieks of laughter slam into me and disperse the panic that keeps me trapped in my nightmare. I know that chorus... intimately. Rage displaces my fear. I buck and thrash. My clawing hands curl into equally impotent fists.

The blankets swaddle me, trapping my hands by my side. What little breath I have is forced from my chest. My mouth gaps, but draws in only foul cotton, rather than dank air. I go still and taut. Struggling only binds me tighter. Atop the thin cover, a weight pins me to the bed; that weight, in turn, holds a pillow across my face. I twist in my involuntary cocoon, my body in one direction and my face the other. I manage an insufficient breath. One final, massive heave and I dump the night hag to the floor. The blanket tears from where she has tucked it beneath the cot. The already-frayed edges shred as I scramble from the tangle and plant my back against the corner wall. The chill creeps through my thin shirt and into my bones. Will alone suppresses the shivers traveling up my spine.

Malice hisses from the narrow strip of floor. I hear the scrape of claws upon concrete as the hag rights herself. I brace for attack, my muscles taut and ready, my chin lowering.

My vision adjusts to the meager light from the corridor outside my cell. At least enough to see the form crouched on the floor, faintly striped by bars of low light and shadow. The binding runes scribed about her neck—the ones that bind her to her cell—have been blurred, the surrounding flesh blistered. Someone has given the hag a brief reprieve, allowing her out to play. For a while, anyway... The lines of the symbols are starting to sharpen once more. Soon the compulsion written into her flesh will repair itself and force her to return to her confinement.

My attention goes back to the familiar features of the one on the floor. One catlike eye stares out from a lined face just above a jaw outthrust and vaguely leonine; the other eye is lost in a marbling of scar tissue that obscures half the hag's face and leaves wide furrows to wrap around her head and through her straggly yellow hair.

I snarl and visualize my fingers making those wounds bleed again. I can see in my mind's eye, my nails leaving fresh marks across that hideous face. My anger demands her other eye. But that is wrong; my anger does not rule me.

"This treachery gains you nothing, Kala," I growl, keeping my voice low, as not to draw the attention of the guards. "You'll still be dogsbody to all the others."

Kala hisses at the double insult.

This is a test. I am new on the Block and my rebellion is a constant challenge. I am not as ruthless, as vicious as the others, just stronger. Smarter. And luckier, perhaps. Definitely more determined. So far, I refuse to be buried beneath the coils of the prison hierarchy. I do not challenge, but neither do I bow down. No one much likes that. Too bad.

A sound from the corridor ends the stalemate. The thud of heavy footsteps on concrete draws closer. The hag shrinks in upon herself. She becomes more catlike in size and posture and slides out between the bars of my cell. The guard stomps by just moments later, intent on something other than me. He doesn't yell, so he hasn't noticed Kala either.

Where is he headed then? What mischief is about? Had Kala been meant to make me a diversion? If so, whoever had helped her blur the runes will be furious. I unfold myself from the corner and creep nearer the bars. More guards hurry past in the direction of the first. The phantom scent of singed hair grows stronger. Not a part of the nightmare, then. In a cell nearby someone has burned. My hands clench and I swallow hard. I press close to the bars in an effort to see what I can of the Block.

Most of it is beyond my view. The cells I can see are steeped in darkness, the corridors hardly brighter. I catch furtive shifting in the shadows and know no one sleeps. They wait and watch. I catch the barest hint of an orange flicker reflecting off the grey cinder-block walls to my left. The smell of burning flesh intensifies.

Two cells down there is a *whoosh*, followed by a roar. The sullen, smoldering glow flares with an infernal intensity. I flinch away and release the bars of my cell, half expecting them to burn me. I hear the laughter of the guards and fall back further into the shadow.

"Another flamer! It's almost getting boring."

"Oh, right," one gravelly voice grumbles. "That's why you're the first to claim your slot in the Pool, yeah?"

"You're just chapped because he always takes the one you have your eye on," another guard laughs, "and mostly wins."

"But what I want to know," the first guard says, ignoring the jab. "Is what happened to the variety?"

"What do you expect? Once they give up hope, it's over. And they all pretty much believe in the same version these days, however much they believe at all…"

"Enough, already."

Hearing this last voice, I slip back under the thin covers and turn toward the wall. The voice belongs to Cerb, the guard in charge of the night shift. I lay there in the dark and strain my ears, hoping to hear the voices recede down the corridor. Instead, the footsteps stop outside my cell. I grit my teeth and fight for stillness, for the illusion of sleep. It is no good.

"Rouse a clean-up crew, starting with this one, seeing as she's awake," Cerb orders before she disappears down the corridor.

I flinch.

My cell opens with the grate of metal on stone. I roll to a sitting position as the bars clang against the end of their track. Before the guards can enter the cell to 'rouse' me, I am at the entrance waiting for instruction, my face impassive. I know better than to give them cause to dispense worse treatment than they will already. The guards are massive, three times the breadth and height of a mortal man, though only twice the size of me. Even so, I keep my gaze averted, vague. I reserve my defiance for my fellow damned and leave the devils alone.

As I stand there, the guard closest to me reaches out an enormous, thick-skinned hand. His flesh is the charcoal color that falls between a normal grey and true black. An obsidian claw tips each finger. All but one curls under; the one extended bites into the flesh at my neck and carves a caveat into my binding runes. The wound burns as if the claw tip is salt-coated. My pained hiss brings satisfied grins to the guards' faces. I fight to keep my lip from lifting in an answering snarl. Instead, I look down at the trickle of deep crimson drawn from my bruise-black skin and mentally dub this guard Char-claw. After all, names have power, even those given by another.

"Follow me," Char-claw rumbles. His gaze is flat and hard. Clearly, he hopes I will not comply. I am not stupid, or suicidal, for that matter. I follow him to the cell two down from my own. The other guards break away, each heading for separate cells. A shifting in the shadows tells me those are occupied. The one in front of me is void of movement. No, not empty, though. Past the bars I see the sullen glow of embers in the process of dying. I swallow hard. Char-claw mutters something and a dull light fills the cell. The bars rattle open, but I go no closer, nor will I, until I am ordered.

Before the other guards return with the rest of the detail, I force myself to stare at the ashen outline of a body delineated on the unmarred cot. The term 'blast-shadow' comes to mind... only this has substance. I clamp down on the urge to retch. I can already feel the fine, clinging motes coating my skin. My throat clogs with the ash that has yet to fill the air. I grit my teeth and force the phantom sensations away. I must impose control before

I begin to feel my flesh crisp and end up screaming my weakness to my adversaries.

The clang of cells opening sounds behind me. A sharp-drawn breath follows shortly, chased by the guards' mocking laughter. Someone has not borne the marking well.

I feel the hard, discouraging expression I have cultivated around the other inmates automatically settle into place as they approach. My transformation does not go unnoticed. Several feet away, Char-claw smirks and flexes the finger with which he had marked me. Fresh agony spears from the gash. I set my teeth against making a sound, then hold my breath and wait out the pain.

He seems mildly amused at the neutral gaze I turn to him. There is a taut moment between us. Then one of my fellow inmates mutters petulantly from inside the cell. "All of us... for this?"

It is Kala.

Kala is an idiot.

Char-claw looks away from me. The pain from my wound instantly fades to a dull ache, but I do not relax. My eyes remain trained upon the guard and his expression. Yes. Kala is definitely an idiot.

He takes one step forward. The hag instinctively cringes down, cowering by the cot. Char-claw sneers and his long arm snaps forward and angles up. The talons rake Kala across her withered chest. Blood sprays the walls of the cell and flicks upon all of us outside, a warm, salty sprinkle that burns like acid. Kala shrieks and crumbles to the floor, whimpering at the further ruin of her body, trembling in shock. I wait for the light to die in her eyes, but they continue to smolder as blood pools about her on the floor.

The guard's hand lashes out again and Kala's hatred flees, replaced by terror. She collapses upon herself, a small, shaking mound huddling on the floor. A high-pitched keen fills the cell. Char-claw laughs as he snags the sheet from the cot, sending the ashes billowing into the air.

"That should be enough to keep all of you occupied," he sneers as he thrusts the sheet toward the inmate behind me. "Bind her wounds with that and get her to work.

"You!" he snaps, with a look in my direction. "Fetch the cleaning supplies."

I gladly back away, turning at the last minute, waiting to feel his claws score my flesh once more. The blow does not come. My head jerks back as if it had, though, upon seeing who else makes up the detail. I do not recognize the slight figure tucked back among the shadows, but the other, her I know all too well. The guards have roused Deth, the self-proclaimed ruler of the Block. Her fists clench on the sheet Char-claw had thrust at her. Her small, poison-yellow eyes snap from Kala to me as I head for the closet at the end of the corridor where the mops and rags and cleaners are locked away. I can feel her displeasure twine around my limbs, dragging down upon me in a constant effort to subdue, to make me subservient. I flex those muscles and release my grip on the rage flowing through me. The threads of her will burn away and I hear her furious hiss. I do not look back.

I start down the corridor, one of the other guards shadowing me, treading close enough to catch my heels at every step. This one is Char-claw's double in all but the color of his skin, which is purplish red, like a blood-engorged cock. That—and his attitude—earns him the name The Dick. His breath is hot and heavy on my neck. I clench my teeth and force myself not to whirl on him like a cornered wolverine. I stop facing the closet, just to the side so he can unlock it.

My "shadow" continues forward until I find myself pinned to the wall. I buck and snarl the instant I feel trapped. His hand snakes around to crush my breast in a brutal grope and he moans into my ear, "Oh yeah, that's right... I love it that you fight." Then The Dick earns his name even more as he laughs and presses his groin tight against my ass. Only threadbare fabric shields me.

I go still, but for a faint trembling I cannot control. My jaw clenches tight against many curses as I struggle to distance myself inside, because there is no hope of doing so physically. The guard laughs again. His tongue flicking out and across my cheek. Thick and sinuous, it strafes my flesh until it stings.

"You had a little something there... a bit sour, but then, it wasn't yours, was it? A pity, that." I jerk in disgust as I realize he has licked Kala's spattered blood from my skin.

His tongue slides over me again, dipping into my ear suggestively. I cannot hold back my shudder. He moans in appreciation and grinds his crotch against me harder, as if he would impale me through our clothes. He reaches around with his other hand to grab me harshly between my thighs.

Even the trembling stops. I go tense and wooden, waiting for the pain.

"Hey!" Char-claw calls from down the corridor. "She's out to clean up, not play. This is already going to take too long, thanks to this one here." There is a thump, and Kala moans. "You want to be the one to explain to Cerb why this is taking all night?"

"Aw, man... come on, this one fights it so good! Just a little... you can even watch."

I force myself not to fight him. It will only goad him on, encourage him to disregard Char-claw's order. The other guard is silent. All I can hear is the heavy panting of The Dick behind me and Kala's continual whimpering. How ironic that earlier she'd tried to kill me only to be my possible salvation now. I hold myself so rigid I feel like stone, no movement but my steady, controlled breaths as I wait for Char-claw's judgment.

"Don't care what you do after orders are carried out, but for now quit screwing around."

The Dick lets out a deep chuckle and grinds himself harder against me, grinding until even my bones threatened to give beneath his thrust. "Soon, then, soon I'll do that lovely ass right." His hand sweeps up away from my breast to brush across my cheek in a deceptively gentle caress that ends in a flick from his razor-edged claw. My head rings with his moan as his tongue flickers out to catch the trail of fresh blood. I swallow hard, fighting revulsion and rage in equal measure.

"Mmmm..." he murmurs once more for my ear alone. "Now *that* is sweet. Can't wait to try out the rest."

My breath comes fast and shallow. I shudder ever so slightly. It has nothing to do with fear; I struggle not to lash out. The Dick finally unlocks the closet and I gather the necessary supplies, my expression blank and my eyes lowered.

The other guards and inmates watch as the two of us make our way back to the cell. The odor of blood and ash assails me from two cells down. I close my mind to the stench and tell myself no dust clogs my throat. Deth grabs for the thick-handled broom the moment I draw close. I tighten my grip on the mop and thrust the bucket and rags to the unfamiliar inmate, ignoring Kala, who is useless even without injuries.

"Here, we'll need water."

The other inmate looks at me with a gaze as dark and deep as forever but does not take the supplies I hold out to her. Her expression bears no malice, no defiance I can see, only surprise. I give her the eye. Where does she come from? I know every inmate here like I know my own face. She is a stranger, unfamiliar. Her pale skin seems to glow like something pure and good against the backdrop of the hellhole surrounding us. She seems distinctly out of place. Of course, I have learned that a pleasant package on the outside is just as likely to hide a rotten core. Hard to say if that is the case here. There is something else off about her though that I cannot pinpoint. I try, but she speaks, and her words distract me. They sound far-off, as if she is not even here.

"Hasn't this gone on long enough?"

My lip curls. As innocent as she sounds, apparently this pale, insubstantial wraith thinks she is going to mess with me, and I will just take it. She reminds me of my brother, Payne. The features are different, obviously, but the attitude is the same. Of course, my brother is dead... because of me. Because I failed to protect him... because I'd been angry over one of his mind games. I'd had to watch as he burned.

I do not like the reminder.

"Just take the friggin' bucket and fill it with water." I snarl. "They tagged you for this detail, and you'll pull your weight like the rest of us."

She ignores my words. "Aren't you ready to come home?"

"Oh, yeah, right!" I spit at her, rattling the bucket with a hard shake. "What are you, my conscience? Water! Now!"

Behind me, I hear Deth laugh, followed by two warm, wet streams drenching the back of my hand and pelting the wooden sides of the bucket. I give the Wraith a black look as the bottom of the container fills with rancid piss.

Char-claw and The Dick burst out laughing as they shake the final drops off their cocks and slip them back into their pants. "Now fill it up right before we finish filling it for you."

I shoot a brutal look toward the Wraith, silently promising retribution, as I never have before. I am shoved from behind hard enough to slop the contents of the bucket down my legs. It is getting harder to keep silent. And harder still not to whirl upon my persecutors.

"Now!" Char-claw roars. "Before I change my mind about letting my buddy here play first."

I move in tight, angry steps toward the crude basin set in the cell wall. It serves double duty as both sink and squatter. I lean the mop against the wall and dump the piss down the bowl, sloshing in some soap, then refilling the bucket with hard, rusty water. The soap fizzes, leaving a thin, skuzzy film across the surface. Like this shithole will ever be clean anyway. We are on this detail just to add to the hell of our existence.

I turn and Deth is behind me, mucking up my mop, swirling it in the splotches of blood and ash. The patterns that form are disturbing, but not as disturbing as the look on her face. Talk about malice. She strokes the handle of the mop suggestively and looks me up and down. Her lip curls in a sneer and her tongue flicks along the edge of her teeth.

"You think you're better than all of us, don't you? Don't you believe it, slut," Deth hisses, her mottled skin rippling as she gets up in my face. "You'll lift your ass for him; just like the rest, you'll take it. And whether you fight or not, you're giving him what he wants.

"He's gonna teach you your place, and when he's done, I'm gonna remind you what it is every chance I get." She strokes the handle once more, ending the motion a foot down the length. The look in her eyes goes bright and lethal as she flexes her powerful wrist. The wood snaps and she slides the short piece into her pants, never taking her eyes off mine. She pats where it lays along her inner thigh, and then reaches out as if to stroke my cheek.

I jerk back with a snarl. Deth just laughs and rubs the bulge again. "This here's for you... you think about that, think about it a lot, sweetheart. You weren't smart enough to drop dead, so now you're gonna be my bitch, after he's had his fun."

She lets go of the mop, which falls against my chest. Reflexively, I grab it, before the guards notice, covering the splintered end with my fist. Deth laughs again and takes up her unblemished broom, turning her back on me as if I am no threat. I struggle not to leap forward and show her how wrong she is. My hand crushes the remaining mop handle until the sound of grinding wood fills the cell.

Five minutes... five minutes alone together and Deth will never again haunt me. I fight the urge. My gaze drifts across the blood spatters and ash. It travels fleetingly over the guards, bullshitting outside the cell. I will not bring myself down to this. I refuse to let them twist me into something vicious and brutal. A few deep breaths and the application of much will power disperses the tide of fury threatening to overwhelm me.

The Dick never does get to... *play.*

By the time we mop up the blood and ash, restoring the cell to its former lackluster state, Cerb returns.

"What's taking so long?" she rumbles.

I stand silently in the back. My hand hides the damaged mop handle from her view. I watch without staring as her dark ebony eyes scan the restored, uniform grey of worn stone, dingy mattress, and iron bars. Her hard gaze sharpens as it draws down once more on where we stand, coming to rest upon Char-claw. I try to read the expression in her flat, muscular face, looking for a clue in the widening jaw that gives this guard the unreadable look of a pit bull. All I can be sure of is I do not want her attention focused on me. I get the impression from the tick in Char-claw's jaw that he shares my sentiment.

"The crew took some persuading."

"Well, they've persuaded themselves out of their morning meal; breakfast hour is over. Get them down to the Yard."

Silently, I gather the cleaning supplies, hiding the broken handle behind the bristles of the up-turned broom. With my arms unavoidably laden, I fall in behind the guards as they lead us from the cell. Deth follows close behind me. It takes an effort to not clench my jaw as my neck bristles in reaction to the enemy at my back. I slow as we near the supply closet, waiting for The Dick to open it once more. My nemesis closes the distance. She comes to a halt right behind me, with not a breath of space between us. The hard bulge of the broken-off handle nestles along my ass. She starts to roll her hips in clear mimicry of The Dick's earlier assault. With a fierce scream I arch away from her and spin around, my fist slamming into her jaw before I can even think. The first crunch is satisfying.

The second: agony.

I roll my head back carefully and look up from the crumpled mound I have become on the corridor floor. The blow had hit hard and fast out of nowhere. I turn empty eyes toward Deth, skimming over her like she is nothing, and settle my gaze on Cerb's cudgel. So, that is what hurt like a motherfucker.

"Seems you make a habit of defacing prison property." Her tone is cold and intractable. Her eyes glide to the side. I look in the same direction and see the mop, fully visible at Deth's feet, and shake my head, more to clear it, than in denial.

Whack! Another smack from the cudgel and my jaw becomes a conduit for the electric fire shooting down my spine. A hand locks on my collar and yanks my head up until I stare Deth in the face. Her expression is filled with contrived pain, its falseness betrayed by the glimmer of satisfaction lurking in the far depths of her eyes.

"Every inmate in this place is prison property," Cerb rumbles low and menacing, like the precursor to a landslide. "You do not damage the goods, understood?"

My gaze flickers from the thin tendril of blood snaking down Deth's jaw to the blood-soaked sheet wrapping Kala's chest. I can feel more than a trickle trailing down my neck. Apparently the guards can break their own toys, but heaven help anyone else that even scuffs them. I clench my jaw and fight down my fury, internalizing the infernal burn. Letting it show would be like placing a weapon in Deth's hand or begging Cerb to strike me down again. Neither bitch needs any help from me.

"Understood?" The cudgel unsubtly rose.

"Yes."

"Put this shit away and get down to the Yard," Cerb orders as she nudges the fallen supplies. Her eyes linger a moment on the ragged end of the mop handle, but she says nothing more.

The Yard.

I hate it.

The Yard is where Deth and her rivals hold Court. Deth rules her Block ruthlessly and against any opposition, as did the others. They have to or they will be pulled down. That's why I piss Deth off. I never really challenge her; I merely decline to play prison politics. For that very reason I stand in the way of her supreme rule.

Tough shit.

As I enter the Yard two things catch my eye: Deth holding Court over by the far wall, and the Wraith lurking by the prison door, closely watching everything going on. What I am about to do breaks a taboo, but I do not much care to be polite at the moment. I stalk over to the Wraith and bring my face down to hers. "Welcome to Hell... what did you do to end up here?"

"This isn't Hell," she answers softly, ignoring my antagonism. "It's Purgatory. Don't let them tell you any different because you aren't damned... yet. You just think you are." The look she gives me is intent. Her eyes shimmer with purity and compassion—neither of which I buy—and her lips draw down ever so slightly in a frown. "You balance on the edge. That's why they push you so hard."

A harsh bark of laughter slips past my lips. "Well, isn't that a nice and delusional analogy, next thing you know, you'll be telling me everything is really sunshine and posies and this is a bad dream." With a sneer tugging at my mouth, I turn my back on her and make my way to the far corner, away from Deth and away from the Wraith and as alone as I can be in a crowded prison yard.

I wipe my face of expression and settle back to watch the show. No doubt there will be one, there always is of some sort or another. Posturing and power plays abound. I might not participate, but I would be a fool to ignore the subtle shifts going on around me.

The crowd around Deth is thick this day. They hover like crows outside a slaughterhouse. Some shift closer, craning their necks in rapt and eager fascination. Others stand taut and still, their eyes darting uneasily away and back again, as if they watch in spite of themselves. The murmurs of the crowd reach me clear across the courtyard. The sound of something hard repeatedly slamming something soft follows, entwining with pained gasps that fall away to whimpers.

My head goes up and my shoulders tense. With each hit the wounds gained by Cerb's hand throb in sympathy. My flaring nostrils draw the tang of copper from the air until I taste it on my tongue. I cannot see it for myself, but blood is being drawn, spattering in the dust of the Yard. Clotting the air. Shrieks rise high. Familiar shrieks.

Kala... paying for her failure. Paying for her stupidity with the guards. Paying for each breath I continue to draw and the rape I have so far escaped.

My jaw grinds with a sound like rock crushing rock. Tension sings through my limbs and I find myself stepping away from the wall. Kala suffers because of me. She might very well die in the dust surrounded by the ghouls watching on. I have been here before, faced with this conflict. I take a step forward as guilt again twists my gut.

No! She tried to kill me last night; she will try again if she survives Deth's beating. So what if she has, for now, saved me from The Dick; that was through her own stupidity, rather than any purposeful effort on her part. I force myself to relax, to remain where I am.

I owe Kala nothing.

I tell myself that over and over, yet what I hear are the Wraith's words drifting through my thoughts like mist rising from the moist ground: *You aren't damned... yet.* Not yet. I try to remind myself she is delusional. Like I have any reason to believe her. Knowing my own sins, belief is nearly impossible. But believe her or not, and no matter my offenses in the past, I am not like the others: I defend myself against the bullies... I do not strike down those who are weaker.

Nor do I have it in me to stand by while others do so.

My determined stride carries me forward. I have pretended it is not so, but all along I have let Deth rule my actions, just like she does all the others. With a menacing growl rumbling in my throat, I push my way through the crowd. I am hardly aware as they close ranks behind me. The scene at the center of the makeshift arena holds all of my attention. Deth stands with legs spread wide and arm raised, the length of mop handle fisted in her hand, ready to backhand Kala.

I cannot suppress my gasp. My body clenches, taut with tension. Kala lies like a puddle on the ground, more pulp than person. Only the sound of her whistling breath betrays the fact that she is still alive.

Great. Another one who reminds me of Payne.

"Enough!" Guilt and anger crackle in my voice.

Deth lowers her improvised cudgel. The crowd falls silent.

"Looks like I'm the one who gets the pleasure of teaching you your place, after all." She slides toward me and strikes lightning fast. I block the blow with one arm and slam my other fist into her jaw.

Our audience gasps and I allow contempt to flow across my expression. "You teach me what *not* to be, nothing more."

I move across the clearing, placing myself between her and Kala. Inmates from all over the Yard start drifting closer to join those from our Block. The leaders push to the fore, with those they rule gathering behind.

Tension crackles through the crowd as everyone waits for the balance of power to shift. I know better. The power does not shift... the focus does. Some of Deth's people creep forward and I tense. I can take a few of them at once, but not the entire Block.

Those that rule the other Blocks clear their throats and move as one to intervene. I have not been here long, but certainly long enough to know they view this as a challenge and if Deth cannot hold her power against me alone, the others will not allow her to hold it with the help of her "subjects".

I curse Kala silently. I want no part of the power plays that drive prison society, but now I have no choice. I should have ignored Deth's punishment circle, but no matter how treacherous Kala is, she does not deserve such brutality.

Deth, obviously, disagrees.

My adversary launches herself across the distance separating us. The rounded end of the stick slams into my gut before I can move. I ignore the pain and grab Deth's wrist, twisting it hard.

She shrieks. Her eyes glow with hatred as she strikes at me with her other fist. I laugh and shove her away. She rages and the crowd shifts. Deth spits at me. Where she strikes bare skin, my arm burns. The muscles beneath tingle until all sensation deadens. I curse and scrub the spot against the tail of my shirt. She makes to spit again, and I backhand her. An angry hiss splits the air and Deth launches a physical attack engaging everything from fists and improvised cudgel to her powerful legs. I evade what I can and bear the blows that strike with an empty expression, giving her nothing. She makes to pummel my face with the wooden cudgel. I pull back only to gasp with shock: a ribbon of agony slices down my cheek. Burning drops fall from my jaw and the smell of fresh blood floods my senses. I roar and lunge at her. Sheer mass on my side, I bear her to the ground. My fists slam into her repeatedly before I tear the mop handle from her grasp. The other end has been worked to a vicious point. I growl and my grip flexes on the length of wood.

My nerves are taut, and my ears catch sounds of movement around me. Pinning Deth to the ground with one massive hand wrapped around her throat and the weight of my body crushed against her torso, I turn my head to gauge the secondary threat.

Our clearing has grown smaller.

I give the crowd a quelling look. Let them see the menace swirling beneath my skin. A wave of unease sweeps through them. I take in the nervous shifting, stare down a few baleful glares. I turn my gaze back toward Deth. "Kala is off limits; you've punished her enough."

Deth chuckles low and evil. Triumph lights her eyes and her thin, hard lips tweak in a dismissive smirk. "You think so, do you?"

Behind me a sick, muffled thud sounds. It is followed by a crunch, and by cruel laughter. I twist around, my hand tightening reflexively upon Deth's throat. Her henchmen have crept in to carry out her bidding while my attention has been on their leader. My eyes lock on Kala's slack face, her lifeless eye. Blood trails down her chin from the corner of her mouth. Payne's face superimposes itself over the macabre sight, like a phantom floating in my mind's eye, damning me. I scream and gnash my teeth. Rage trembles through my limbs and hope flees before it. I am finally damned in truth. I have failed once more to protect. It has never been my strong suite.

But vengeance... I am *real* good at vengeance.

I loosen my grip on the makeshift cudgel until the blunt end is in my palm and the sharpened end is clear. Intent fills my eyes: anger, rage, vengeance, malice... I allow all of that to flow through me until my raised arm vibrates with their dark power.

Down it plunges, buried all the way to the blunt end in my nemesis's chest. Blood pools around my fingers, searing them. The tingling burn travels up my arm and straight to my heart, where all sensation dies.

I stand. Taking up my new mantle, I turn damned eyes upon my new subjects.

"I am Deth... bow down before me."

About the Author

Award-winning author, editor, and publisher Danielle Ackley-McPhail has worked both sides of the publishing industry for longer than she cares to admit. In 2014 she joined forces with husband Mike McPhail and friend Greg Schauer to form her own publishing house, eSpec Books (www.especbooks.com).

Her published works include six novels, *Yesterday's Dreams, Tomorrow's Memories, Today's Promise, The Halfling's Court, The Redcaps' Queen,* and *Baba Ali and the Clockwork Djinn,* written with Day Al-Mohamed. She is also the author of the solo collections *Eternal Wanderings, A Legacy of Stars, Consigned to the Sea, Flash in the Can, Transcendence, Between Darkness and Light, The Fox's Fire, The Kindly One,* and the non-fiction writers' guides *The Literary Handyman, More Tips from the Handyman,* and *LH: Build-A-Book Workshop.* She is the senior editor of the Bad-Ass Faeries anthology series, *Gaslight & Grimm, Side of Good/Side of Evil, After Punk,* and *Footprints in the Stars.* Her short stories are included in numerous other anthologies and collections.

In addition to her literary acclaim, she crafts and sells original costume horns under the moniker The Hornie Lady Custom Costume Horns, and homemade flavor-infused candied ginger under the brand of Ginger KICK! at literary conventions, on commission, and wholesale.

Danielle lives in New Jersey with husband and fellow writer, Mike McPhail and two extremely spoiled cats.

Those We Shall Spare

Anders Håkon Gaut
Anonymous Reader
Aysha Rehm
C.J. Frost
Cato Vandrare
Cheri Kannarr
Christopher J. Burke
Christopher Weuve
Chuck Robinson
Deanna Stanley
eSpec Books
Gary Phillips
Gav
Heather Stephens
Ian Harvey
James Gotaas
Jaq Greenspon
Jen Kappert

Jennifer L. Pierce
Judi Fleming
Judith Waidlich
Kelly Pierce
L.E. Custodio
Lark Cunningham
Lorraine J. Anderson
maileguy
mdtommyd
Mike M.
Peter Engebos
pjk
Scott Schaper
Steph Parker
Stephen Ballentine
The Creative Fund
Tina M Noe Good